DEAD WEIGHT

ALSO BY

HILDUR KNÚTSDÓTTIR

The Night Guest

HILDUR KNÚTSDÓTTIR

TRANSLATED BY

MARY ROBINETTE KOWAL

NIGHTFIRE

TOR PUBLISHING GROUP • NEW YORK

DEAD WEIGHT

Translation by Mary Robinette Kowal

A Nightfire Book
Published by Tom Doherty Associates / Tor Publishing Group
120 Broadway
New York, NY 10271

www.torpublishinggroup.com

Nightfire™ is a trademark of Macmillan Publishing Group, LLC.

EU Representative: Macmillan Publishers Ireland Ltd, 1st Floor, The Liffey Trust Centre, 117–126 Sheriff Street Upper, Dublin 1, D01 YC43

The Library of Congress Cataloging-in-Publication Data is available upon request.

ISBN 978-1-250-32929-5 (hardcover)
ISBN 978-1-250-32930-1 (ebook)

First published as *Gestir* in 2025 in Iceland by Forlagið.

First U.S. Edition: 2026

Printed in the United States of America

10 9 8 7 6 5 4 3 2 1

DEAD WEIGHT

PROLOGUE

I have thought long and hard about how I would dispose of a dead body. I have carefully weighed options such as digging, sinking, burning, hiding. It's something I do when I can't sleep. I used to think that everyone did this, that each person I met had a plan of their own. But the day I casually mentioned mine during lunch at work, a weird and uncomfortable silence settled over the table. So it turns out that most people listen to audio books when they can't sleep. It's only me who hides bodies. I find it relaxing.

It has taken me years to perfect my plan. I never thought that I would actually have to put it into motion. But that just goes to show how the river of life sometimes insists on taking unexpected turns, no matter how hard you have worked on forging a neat forward path for it. And I have worked *so hard*.

As the saw cuts into the meaty flesh of a muscled forearm, I wonder if Io somehow sensed this about me. Was that the reason she came? Did she know my knives are always sharp?

I have imagined this process so many times. But one thing does surprise me. I've barely begun and my hands are already hurting. I put the saw down and flex my fingers before starting on the bone.

1

I forgot the reusable bag. I always forget the damn reusable bag. And I don't know what I hate more: stiff paper bags or those disgustingly thin biodegradable plastic bags that always tear immediately. The grips on both cut into your palms. But I can*not* be one of those people who walks around with a backpack. Only teenagers and tourists do that. Not thirty-three-year-old business analysts who work on Borgartún—not ones who work in *the very center* of Reykjavík's financial district.

It was only as I was clocking out from work that I remembered that I needed groceries. I had gotten back late from the airport the night before, and my fridge was completely empty. I had thought about going home to get the car, but decided to stop on the way and just get the essentials. I didn't realize how much I had in my basket until it was in the bags. There were only paper bags at Bónus, so now I'm holding one in each hand, and my palms are already sore from the stiff handles. Thirty-three-year-old business professionals working on Borgartún don't have calluses. We have soft hands.

I'm out of breath as I walk up through Grjótaþorpið, the oldest part of the city, and the back of my neck is damp. I must reek of sweat. I need a shower. Do I have any clean laundry?

The steps outside my front door creak. I live in a small three-story wooden house that was built in 1907 by a sea captain for his family, but has now been turned into three flats. I live on the middle floor. The wood of the steps outside my door is probably as old as the house, but I've lived here for eight years and never had a problem with rot. I have to put my bags down to fish the key out of my coat pocket. I open the door, kick off my shoes, and put the bags on the kitchen table. I throw off my coat and hurry into the bedroom, scooting past the suitcase that sits in the middle of the floor where I'd put it last night before collapsing into bed. I've got to get out of this cashmere sweater before I die of heatstroke. Wadding it up, I toss it into the closet. Then I head to the living room but freeze in my tracks.

There is a cat lying on my couch.

It is small and compact, with black on its back and on the top of its head. There is a red collar around its neck but no tag. It turns its white belly to me and looks at me with half-closed eyes.

I don't have a cat.

"Who are you?" I ask.

The cat twitches its tail, and then it starts purring; I can hear it all the way across the room where I stand by the door, staring at it.

"Out. Out!" I say. Then I flap my hands to show that

it's not welcome. The cat narrows its green eyes again. Is it falling asleep?! This is *not* acceptable.

I stride to the cat and pick it up.

The fur is incredibly soft and reminds me of the inside of the leather gloves that Jói gave me for Christmas two years ago. Every time I wear them, I try not to think about the rabbit that had to die for the gloves. The cat is still purring, and now I can feel the rumble under my fingers and palms and up against my ribs where the cat's back touches my chest. The cat vibrates like a cell phone, and the sensation unleashes something inside of me that I can't name. Something so sweet it hurts.

I open the front door and set the cat down on the steps. It looks up at me and meows. There is a question in its tone.

"You don't belong here," I say.

Then I close the door in its face.

When I've put away the groceries, I unpack my bag. It doesn't take me long. If you pack your bag right it's easy to unpack. I am very good at packing bags. I have a special system and an excellent eye for what fits where. Jói couldn't believe it the first time we went away together. A shiver of pleasure runs through me as I remember the look on his face when he saw just how much I could fit in a carry-on suitcase. It's nice to have someone in your life who appreciates your talents.

I sit on my sofa—luckily the cat didn't shed any fur—and call Jói. He answers after three rings.

"Yes?"

The question is short. I can immediately tell that he can't speak. But I need to talk to him.

"Hi."

"What?"

I hear children's voices in the background.

"They're not at school?" I ask.

"No. Teacher workday."

"Oh. Okay. Listen, I just got word today that the meeting I was telling you about? It's tomorrow. And I wanted to run some ideas past you."

I can hear from the silence on the other end of the line that he doesn't remember. My heart shrinks, as if it's trying to hide in my chest.

"With Þorvard. The director. I mentioned it over dinner the day before yesterday; remember? At that pasta place."

"I can't talk now."

"Can you call tonight?"

There is silence on the line again. The silence means no. I wonder if he thinks it hurts me less than saying the word?

"Jói. I just want to go over this a little bit. There's no one else I . . ."

"We're not interested," he says, his voice changing suddenly. He's speaking to me like a stranger, his performance so believable that it hurts. Then he hangs up.

I stare out the window. I wonder how my name is listed in his phone's contacts. He's never told me and I've never asked.

A little voice in the back of my mind whispers that maybe it's not even listed there at all. I hurry to silence it before it says anything else.

I go to the kitchen and start dinner. I push my knife through the carrots slowly. I enjoy the sounds they make, like fingers breaking under my blade.

It's not until I'm lying in bed in the dark trying to fall asleep that I wonder how the cat actually got in.

2

I wake up forty minutes before my alarm goes off. Partly because of the stress about the meeting with Þorvard. Tumi has been sick lately. And there have been whispers that it's something serious and that they are going to need a replacement. Tumi manages the entire marketing department. This is a huge job. I was recently asked to take over the implementation of the new web interface on our customer service website, which Tumi has otherwise handled. And now Þorvard wants to review how it went. He's the type to ask you questions about all sorts of random things in meetings without giving you time to prepare. He's one of those people who think that the first reaction is usually the right one. Which is, of course, pure nonsense. Good ideas come later, when you have thought about the problem—and it's best to give the subconscious a few days to do its work. The subconscious is like the mice in Cinderella. Go to bed at night and they do the work for you while you sleep.

The first reaction is the learned one. Prejudice. So you have to correct the biases in yourself. Þorvard, like a lot of men, has just never had to.

It must be wonderful to travel through life as a tall

white man. To have a deep voice. Big hands. Strong, confident jaw.

I lie on my back and look at the ceiling above me, making a list in my mind of all the good ideas that I'll pretend to get on the spot if he asks.

I'm going to tell him that I think we can do a better job of cultivating the customers we already have. Instead of always focusing on getting new customers, as Tumi has done, and offering them better terms for changing insurance companies, we should make sure that our existing customers are happy.

We could do better reaching out to younger people.

And I think many things could be simplified on our website.

Also, we must not forget that older people want to be able to talk to human beings, not a chat window.

I practice the look I'm going to use. Raise my eyes up and to the right. Because I've read that people look there when they're doing creative thinking, but to the left when doing recall.

My alarm clock rings.

I sit up and the first thing I notice is the cat, who is curled up on my bed and sleeping soundly.

3

That evening, when I get home from work, the black-and-white cat is once again sitting outside my door. I stop at the bottom of the stairs when I spot it. The cat stands up, swaying its tail and meowing. As if it is saying hello. Like it's happy to see me.

"You couldn't get in this time, I see. Serves you right."

Because it must have gotten in through the kitchen window before. Or possibly the crack in the bathroom window. So I closed both before I went to work and put the cat outside as I left. Has it just been waiting here all day?

I walk up the stairs and the cat meows again. It takes a position at the door and looks up at me. Like it expects me to let it in.

"So long. Shoo," I say. "Scram."

But there's no conviction in my voice. Because I'm thinking about how hungry it must be. The cat must sense that it's found my weak spot, because it meows again, plaintively.

"Fine, then," I sigh. Then I open the door and the cat runs in.

I give it water in a bowl and open a can of tuna. Standing with my arms crossed, I watch it eat its fill. It must have been ravenous. It finishes all the tuna on the plate, so I give it more.

Then I sit in the living room and pick up the phone.

I call Jói. He declines the call after two rings. I get an uncomfortable feeling at the back of my throat but swallow it down.

The cat walks in from the kitchen. It makes a dash toward me, then jumps onto the couch and curls up next to me. It rests its head on my thigh and looks up.

Before I know it, my hand is scratching the cat's head. It closes its eyes again and begins to purr. Then it sticks out its chin, obviously asking for a scratch on its neck. I give it scritches.

It's so warm lying on top of me. I stroke its back. Its fur is silky and shiny. It stretches out its paws and starts kneading my thigh. The feeling from yesterday comes back. Warm and so tender—and I realize how much I miss being touched.

"I just wanted to talk to him," I say to the cat. "And tell him about the meeting."

The cat rolls onto its back and turns its belly up. I scratch it there.

"I just wanted to tell him what Þorvard said."

The cat cracks a green eye and looks at me. Then closes it again, and I wonder if it's asleep.

I study the cat. I can see clearly between *her* legs

as she lies on her back. Someone must miss her. She's obviously not afraid of people, and she seems to be in good shape. She's even a little chubby. Someone has taken good care of her.

I open Facebook and check the neighborhood page. I don't have to scroll long before I get to the ad.

There is a picture of the cat lying next to me. The caption says: *IO IS LOST!!*

The cat, Io, lives on Framnesvegur. She's been missing for two days.

"Io," I say and the cat opens her eyes. "Jupiter's moon? That's a strange name for a cat."

Then I call the phone number the woman posted. Her name is Ásta Ólafardóttir. She answers after one ring.

4

Eight minutes later my doorbell rings. Really, eight minutes exactly. I timed it. When I open the door, Ásta is standing outside, out of breath and cheeks flushed. She must have run. She is wearing an unzipped coat over pajama bottoms and a fleece pullover, and she's holding a cat carrier. Her hair, which is fair and could use a wash, is in a tousled bun on top of her head. The eyes in her pale face are large and blue.

She is beautiful. One of those people who should be a model or actress. But this is a first impression thought, I remind myself. My prejudices talking. Of course, beautiful women can work on whatever they're interested in and want to do, rather than letting their looks dictate their choices. Maybe she is a doctor. Or a diver.

"Hello," I say. "I'm Unnur."

"Ásta," she says. "Is . . . is she here?"

"Yes. Come in."

Ásta steps into the entryway and takes off her scuffed sneakers. Then she follows me into the living room, to the couch where the cat is still lying.

I expect her to follow me over to the couch, and when she doesn't, I look over my shoulder.

Ásta stands in the doorway and stares at the cat. Her big blue eyes seem to have grown by half, and she almost looks like a cartoon character.

"Isn't that her?" I ask.

Ásta covers her mouth. And then I realize that she has started to cry.

"I'm sorry," I say. "I saw the picture and I was sure it was your cat."

Ásta wipes her eyes. Then she rushes to the sofa, drops to her knees and sweeps the cat into her arms. The cat flattens its ears but otherwise seems to tolerate the embrace.

Ásta's shoulders shake as she cries silently.

I hesitate for a moment, and then I turn my back on her and go into the kitchen. I can't watch this. I don't know if it's to give her privacy as she completely loses control, or if I'm just embarrassed about standing there and looking into her soul.

I make tea because that's what you do in a situation like this, right?

I'm relieved when the hum of the kettle fills the air. And I make sure to clink the cups to announce my arrival before I take them out to the living room.

Ásta is sitting on the sofa. The cat has curled up in her lap. Her eyes are red and swollen, but she's stopped crying.

She looks at me. "I'm so sorry. Please, forgive my outburst. I've just missed her so much."

"No problem." I put on a polite smile that I hope is also friendly. I hand her the cup of tea and take a sip of my own. This is a soothing herbal tea. "I understand completely," I say, although of course I don't.

"I've just missed her so incredibly, incredibly much." Ásta blows her nose. "I thought something terrible had happened. That she had been locked away somewhere or that someone had run over her and left her injured on the side of the road, like some piece of junk. And you know, some people have been taking cats from neighborhoods and driving them to completely different neighborhoods!"

"Really?"

"Yes!" she says and is clearly very distressed. "They've even switched out their collars. Who does that?"

This seems like a genuine question. Her big eyes look at me as if I might have some answers—that I might know the kind of men (because they must be men; they are always men) who would do such a thing.

"I don't know," I say.

Ásta looks at me for a moment, as if she is waiting for me to add something. When I don't, she looks back down at the cat.

"And all this time she was here."

"Yeah," I say apologetically.

And then I tell her about last night, that Io was casually lying on my couch when I got home and in my bed when I woke up this morning, and this afternoon she was waiting for me at the front door.

"She must have wandered a little too far and then couldn't find her way home," says Ásta.

I nod, even though I know nothing about cats and their travels. "That must be it."

Ásta is still in her coat, although she does not seem to be leaving any time soon. And she hasn't touched her tea.

My phone starts ringing. It's Jói. A rush of heat washes through me, like it always does when his name appears on my phone.

"Hi," I say.

"Hi, how are you?"

"Just fine. But listen, I can't really talk right now. Can I call you in a bit?"

He is silent for a moment. I try to remember the last time *I* was the one who couldn't talk, but can't.

"No," he says. "I can't talk later."

My heart sinks. I glance at Ásta. She sits, the cup of tea still untouched in her hand, staring at Io. I am filled with the urge to throw both her and her stupid cat out of my apartment and out of my life. But she looks so heartbroken that I am immediately ashamed of the impulse. They'll be gone in a few minutes. The least I can do is be polite.

"Oh," I say. "Are you sure?"

"Yes," he says.

"Okay. Talk to you later."

I hang up, turn back to my guest, and clear my throat.

At that, Ásta winces. "I'm sorry. I must be interrupting."

"No." I put on a polite smile, but it's one of those that I know isn't friendly.

Ásta takes hold of the cat and stands up. She shoves Io into the carrier she brought and locks it. "Thank you so much for calling."

"No problem."

"No, really, thanks." She walks up to me, and to my horror, she takes my hands. Her fingers are thin and cold, like she has poor circulation. She squeezes twice and looks into my eyes as she says, "Thank you."

She means it so sincerely that I blush. How can she walk around so exposed, with an opening into her soul, and allow others to look in? Does she feel no shame?

"No problem," I say. "Really."

I want to snatch my hands back, but that would be rude, so I don't. Ásta squeezes my fingers a third time and then lets go.

She picks up the carrier, and when she turns to me, Io, who doesn't seem to appreciate being in there, lets out a long moan.

"How should I pay you?" she asks.

"What do you mean?" I'm confused.

"For the reward. It was in the post."

I shake my head, but before I can say anything else, she adds: "It's only fourteen thousand ISK. I'm sorry I don't have more. But of course, you deserve it. Because you found her."

"No," I say firmly. "No. Not at all. That's completely unnecessary."

"Are you sure?"

"One hundred percent sure."

"Okay." Then she smiles at me and walks out with the cat.

When I close the door behind them, I feel instant relief.

5

I am alone again, blessedly without a wide-eyed, teary young woman and a stray cat on my pristine white sofa. I look down at my phone, at the record of Jói's call earlier. I wanted to tell Jói that the meeting had gone well. I picture him smiling at the news. "I knew it would," he might have said if that woman and her damn cat hadn't been here.

I'd tell him that we had started by me updating Þorvard on how the implementation of the new web interface had gone, though it had been obvious that he wasn't even really listening as I went over the main points.

But I had pushed on, leading the meeting as if he did care. My moment would come. And finally, Þorvard had nodded, distracted, and then gazed out the window in an obvious attempt to be casual. "Do you have any ideas on the marketing side of things, in general? What has gone well; what could be improved?"

He didn't mention Tumi, his alleged illness, or the potential need to find a replacement for the marketing manager position.

I had furrowed my brow the way I'd practiced,

looked thoughtful, and then looking up and to the right, I had listed the ideas I had come up with. Not all at once though—I made sure to pause occasionally, drawing it out, as if the ideas were coming to me on the spot.

Þorvard had said nothing, but he'd nodded and written some of them down.

I know he'll probably talk to Gummi and Helga, too, but I have a good feeling about this.

The next day passes without a word or a glance from Þorvard. But I know that I can't expect to hear anything yet, so I push my excitement down. If there is anything that I have become an expert in, it's waiting. As my workday ends, it's raining, but I decide to walk home anyway. I hate taking the bus in the rain. The smell of wet coats and teenagers with greasy hair inside an airless carriage is too much for me.

For once there is no wind. The rain is a fine mist, more like fog than precipitation. It condenses on my wool coat, forming tiny droplets that sparkle like crystals. I am about to put on my favorite true crime podcast. It's not one of those sensational, gruesome ones that are only trying to capitalize on other people's misery and seem to be springing up everywhere, even here in Iceland. I was contacted by one a couple of years ago. But I have no interest in exposing my wounds for voyeurs. This podcast isn't agony porn though. It puts crimes in a wider sociopolitical context, is well researched, heavy on the science, and very respectful to those who survived and the families of those that didn't. But as I am about to press play, I decide to try calling Jói instead. He doesn't answer. I didn't really expect him to, but still, it hurts.

I wonder what he's doing. Is he at the gym? Out for a run? Buying groceries? I think about the time when we visited that open air market in Tangier. I remember the smell of spices and sweet ripe fruits, and his big strong hand in mine. We kissed in front of a fountain, and then we bought pears from an old man with a white beard. I had never tasted anything so sweet.

About a minute later, a text message arrives: *I'll talk to you tonight.*

I want to answer him and say: *Sorry, I can't talk then. Busy.*

But, of course, that would be a lie. I don't have any plans tonight except for yesterday's leftover soup and a few episodes of *Love is Blind*.

This is how it's always been with us. He gives when he can and I wait patiently, gratefully accepting what is offered. There was a point when I would get angry and impatient, and once I even broke things off with him after he had to cancel one of our trips while I was already on my way to the airport. I had felt free for about a week. But then, as the days passed, the memories of all the beautiful places we had visited, all the nights that we had spent together, those intimate moments when nothing existed in the world but the two of us, started to crowd in on my mind, like a ceiling getting lower every day. It had dawned on me that I had made a mistake. Jói *knew me*; he had known me instantly, from the very start. Many people spend their whole lives never finding that. It's rarer than striking gold and more precious. I realized then that having just a part of him in my life is better than not having him at all. He gives as much as he can, and things are going to change for the better soon. Good things come to those who wait. I truly believe that.

I hang my coat by the radiator when I get home. Then I go into the bathroom and dry my face. I have decided to reheat the soup before I go out for a run, and set it to simmer on the stove. But I hesitate. There's a strange smell in the air. As if by . . . I frown. I don't quite understand it. But it somehow reminds me of the smell from when my mom and dad used to make blood sausage when I was little. It's the smell of something that should be inside the body but isn't.

I look under the couch.

Nothing there.

Maybe the compost is starting to smell? But I haven't cooked meat in weeks.

I go into the kitchen. The smell is fainter there.

I go back into the living room. Close my eyes and sniff.

The smell is gone. I open my eyes, look around, and the odor hits me again.

Then I spot something on my bed. Something black.

I walk into the bedroom. I made my bed this morning. I always do before I go to work.

In the middle of my bed, the cat Io is curled up into a small furry ball.

"What are you doing now . . ." I trail off when I spot the bloodstain on the bedspread.

Was she hit by a car? And did she sneak in here, injured?

Io looks up. She meows and stretches. It's then that I see the newborn kitten snuggled against her belly.

6

"Oh my god," says Ásta. "Oh my god."

I nod, completely agreeing.

She stares down at the kitten. He is jet-black except for a tiny snow-white star on his chest. His eyes are closed and he is ridiculously small. Ásta's big blue eyes are full of wonder, and her expression is so gentle that I'm filled with embarrassment, but I don't know if it's for her sake or mine.

"I had no idea she was pregnant," she says, shaking her head slowly. "I swear it. She'd gained a little weight, but not that much. I didn't suspect anything! And what is she doing here? Why did she come here to have the kitten?"

"I don't know—"

Ásta interrupts me. "I do everything for her. EVERYTHING. I buy her favorite wet food. Do you know how much it costs?"

"No, I—"

"And then she comes here. To have her kitten."

"Yes, I—"

"Maybe she's upset that . . ." Ásta falls silent, frowns and then bites her lip.

"What?"

But Ásta shakes her head. "Nothing."

"Okay . . ." Although it is obviously not nothing. My curiosity has been piqued. It burns bright, like a sparkler.

Ásta stares down at Io and her kitten. Her palms are clenched.

We both flinch when the phone rings. My heart lurches. Jói. But then I realize it's not my phone. It's the same ringtone, but my phone is on the coffee table, where I put it after I called Ásta. This ringing comes from her coat, which is on the corner of my bed.

Ásta reaches into her coat and picks up the phone. She looks at the screen for a moment. Then she swallows and answers. "Hey, my love. Oh, no, I'm on my way home. I'm just at the store. I was going to buy apples in Pétursbúð but there are none. Not green ones, I mean. No, I mean yes, I'll come home now. Okay. Bye."

Ásta hangs up. Then she looks at me, her blue eyes full of something I can't name. My curiosity burns brighter. But this isn't my business. She is not my business. I just want to get her and this cat out of my life. I clear my throat and look away. My eyes flutter over the cat, the kitten, Ásta's blue coat. And then I realize that she came empty-handed.

I look up.

"Where's the cat carrier?" I ask. "How are you going to get them home?"

Ásta looks at me.

"Unnur," she says. And I can see in her face, hear in her voice, that I am not going to like what she says next. "Unnur, we can't move her now. Newborn kittens need to be in a stable environment. If we move her now, Io might just . . . reject the kitten. She clearly doesn't want to be at home; she doesn't want to be with me . . ." Ásta's voice breaks, it seems to me that she is on the verge of sobbing again, but then she clears her throat and seems to pull herself together. "She didn't want to be at home, Unnur. She chose this place. If I take her, she might try to drag him back here and it's getting cold and I think we're expecting frost. And what if she drops the kitten? He would freeze to death! She wants to be here, at least for now."

I stare at her. She can't be serious. She must be pulling my leg, so I start laughing. But Ásta just looks at me, with such entreaty in her gaze that the laughter dies in my throat, as if someone has turned off the air.

"Wait, are you just going to dump them on me?" I ask.

She flinches, as if I've slapped her. "No! No, not at all!"

"Listen, I really don't have time to deal with a cat."

"I'll clean up after her!" says Ásta. "And I'll bring food; I'm going to buy special food for nursing cats. I'll bring her litter box and her bed and I'll take the poo out and change the litter and clean her bowl. I . . . I may not always be able to make it every day. So, if you could maybe make sure she has access to clean water, if you could maybe just change the water, then . . ."

She falls silent. We stare at each other.

"Only for a few weeks, just until he's a little bit older. Maybe just until he opens his eyes." Then she brightens as if she has the solution. "I'll pay you!"

I shake my head. "It's not about money. A cat is a big commitment and I don't know if I'm ready to . . . I mean, I have my own life; you get that, right?"

"Yes, of course," she says. "Of course. But, just look at her. Look at him. We can't move them."

We both look down at the cat and the kitten. The kitten is nursing. Io lies on her side and makes air biscuits with her paws. She looks up at us and closes her eyes again.

Ásta puts a hand on my shoulder and I look up. "Please do this."

"No," I say.

"Unnur . . ."

"No!"

We look into each other's eyes and I see hers fill with tears.

"Please do this," she says again. I watch the tears flow over her lids and slide down her cheeks in two streams. How is she actually doing this? Making me the bad guy? Tears collect in drops on her delicate jawline and fall onto her shirt. I feel my defenses failing.

I sigh. "Just for a few weeks, you say?"

She nods. Wipes her eyes with the back of her hand. "Just for a very short time. Just while he's getting stronger. Io is very little trouble, I promise. She never meows and she doesn't really shed. And I think kittens sleep a lot in the first few weeks. They're always sleeping. You won't even notice them. And if they damage something, I'll pay for it!"

I look at the bloodstains on the bedspread. That was Egyptian cotton—six hundred threads. What had she planned to pay as a finder's fee for Io? Fourteen thousand ISK? That's less than one of my sheets. I don't need to look at her bank account to know that Ásta can't afford a new set. And it's not as if no one has bled on them before. It's just that you never know if you'll really be able to get the blood out.

"Okay," I say. "Okay."

Ásta's shoulders sag, as if someone has loosened a string. She hugs me.

"Thank you," she whispers in my ear. "Thank you."

Goose bumps rise on my cheeks and neck when I feel her hot breath on my ear. I put my arm around her and clumsily pat her on the back, hoping she'll let me go. But she squeezes me even tighter, so her bony shoulders press against my chest. I pat her shoulder blade. She is scary thin.

She finally releases me and I take a deep breath.

"Thank you," she says for the third time. "This means so much to me."

"No problem," I say, though of course it's not true. I just don't know what else to say.

"But hey . . . would it be okay if I . . . I mean, would it be okay if I maybe come spend a bit of time with them sometimes?"

"Spend time with them?"

She nods. "Yes, just sometimes. I mean, Io . . . it was just the two of us for so long. And I miss her. So I was wondering if maybe I could come over sometimes and have a little visit with her. Just sit with them for a bit and get to know the kitten, too, and let him get to know me. Just so he at least learns to recognize my scent."

I frown. "Um . . . sure. I guess you can do that?"

"Maybe after nine o'clock on Tuesday and Thursday nights and a quarter past eleven on Saturdays?" she blurts. Then takes a deep breath. "A quarter past eleven on Saturday mornings, I mean."

"Is there . . . are those the times that work for you?" I ask.

"Yes," says Ásta.

"Okay," I say. "I think I can make that work, for the most part. Unless something comes up, of course, and I'm busy"

"Absolutely. Of course. Yes, no problem. Then just let me know. But could you maybe text me instead of calling?"

I stare at her for a moment. "Uh . . . sure. No problem."

“Thank you.” Ásta's smile lights her face up like a Christmas star. I'd never seen her smile. She was beautiful before, but when she smiles, she's almost supernatural—like an elf stepping out of her hill. My breath catches in my chest. I cough.

“Are you okay?” Her smile fades and her brow furrows with concern.

“Yeah. Totally fine.”

Her phone rings. She flinches, as if she has been beaten. She reaches for it and answers: “Hey, my love. No, I'm not quite home yet. The weather is so beautiful that I decided to walk along the harbor. Okay. See you in a bit. Bye.”

She hangs up and looks at me. Smiling apologetically. Opens her mouth, as if to explain, but closes it again without saying anything.

My curiosity is red-hot.

She looks down at the cats and strokes Io.

“I need to go. But I'll come tomorrow. With her bed, the litter box, and food.”

“Okay,” I say.

She goes down on her knees, kisses Io on the head. She whispers something to her, but I can't make out the words.

When she's gone, I sit on the bed. Io looks up at me and starts purring. I scratch her under the chin. The kitten seems content and lies fast asleep next to her stomach. He's not really like a cat. His muzzle is almost flat, his eyes are closed, his tiny ears are at the back of his head, and his legs are so short that they're more like buns than paws. He looks more like a tiny seal than a cat.

And then I realize that I won't get Io's bed until tomorrow. Where are they going to sleep tonight? They can't be at my feet. I might kick them in my sleep. And to be honest, I don't really want to sleep with this bedspread. What did Io do with the placenta? I think some animals eat it? At any rate, it's nowhere to be seen.

I lie down on the bed, wrapping my arms around the cat. Feel the warmth from her against my chest and stomach—the vibration of her purr.

I'll put the bedspread in the corner, make a little bed on the floor for them with it. I can sleep with my other blanket, the thick one. The weather is starting to feel like I need to swap them anyway. Maybe it's true what Ásta said about it freezing in the night? Or did she just say that to convince me to say yes?

I pet the sleeping kitten. His coat is thin. I run my fingers along his back. The bones of his spine are like the heads of knitting needles. The skin stretches over his tiny ribs. He is so fragile that I get a lump in my throat.

Io rolls onto her back and pokes her head into the crook of my neck.

"There, there," I say.

My phone rings on the coffee table. I place my hand on Io's chest, feeling her rumble under my palm. Then I stand.

It's Jói. A thrill of excitement runs through me like a current.

"Hi," I say. I can't wait for him to hear about my day.

7

"Is it weird that there's only one kitten?"

"Yes. That's what the vet said, too." Ásta tells me. It's a quarter past nine on a Tuesday night and she's sitting on my bedroom floor, next to Io and the kitten. "And I googled it, too. Sometimes, they can have nine in a litter. But usually it's four to six."

"You called the vet?" I ask, surprised. Although maybe I shouldn't be. It's clear that Ásta really loves this cat.

Ásta had brought Io's bed, placed it in the living room, and brought the kitten there. Io had chased after her, meowing. As soon as Ásta put the kitten down in the bed, Io had picked it up by the nape of the neck, carried him back into the bedroom, and laid him atop the folded blanket. It was funny to see her run with him. He had pulled his legs up to his body and swayed in her mouth as she walked, like a pear.

There are now also yellow stains on the bedspread. I suspect it's piss. Because the kitten can't go to the litter box yet and something has to happen to all that milk he drinks. He spends most of the day nursing.

"Why did you call the vet?" I ask.

"Just to ask for advice. And to try to understand why she decided to have her kitten here and not at home."

"And what did the vet say?"

"That she needed nutritious food and privacy. And plenty of water, of course. If we take care of her, she'll take care of the kitten."

"But what did he say about the other thing?"

"She," Ásta corrects. "I don't think I've ever met a male vet."

"Anyway," I say, not remembering ever meeting a vet. "Did she say anything about why Io didn't give birth at home?"

Ásta pulls her legs up, pressing her thighs against her chest. She wraps her arms around her legs and rests her chin on her knees. "That it happens when cats experience insecurity."

"Okay . . . But insecurity, why? Is there construction happening in the building or something?"

"No," says Ásta. "And she's been with me for almost three years. Since she was a tiny kitten. But . . . but my boyfriend recently moved in."

"Oh," I say.

"And she doesn't like him."

"Apparently," I say, laughing.

But Ásta does not laugh. She looks sad. As if by rejecting her boyfriend, the cat is rejecting her, too.

I'm ashamed for laughing, but it feels stupid to apologize for it, so I don't. "Did you just start dating?"

"No. But he just moved South. He was at sea, in the East Fjords. Then he lost his position. Now he's actively job hunting."

She says "actively job hunting" like it's a job title.

"Gotcha. And . . . is he not nice to her?"

She shrugs. "He's fine. Or, I mean, he mostly pretends he doesn't see her. But maybe it's just the smell of him, having someone new in the apartment. I don't know."

She stares at the cats, sadness written all over her face.

"So what do you do?" I ask.

"I'm in college. In literary studies. I'm in my last year; I'm taking courses now and in the spring I'll write my thesis. And I'm cleaning in the afternoons, at a kindergarten."

"Are you from the East, too?" The East Fjords are beautiful, desolate, and sparsely populated.

She nods. "I came South to Reykjavík because my aunt got sick. She didn't have anyone else, and she needed help with day-to-day stuff. But then she died, and by then I had started school, so I decided to just finish, even though Raggi wanted me to come back East. But I'm so close to graduating, you know? And then he came here. We're trying to save up for a house back home."

"What kind of work is there for literary majors in the East Fjords?" I ask.

Ásta laughs. "What kind of work is there for literary majors anywhere? But I don't know; I'll see. Worst case, nursing homes are always hiring."

I know I'm questioning her. But I'm so curious about this woman who suddenly has visitation rights to my home. I tried googling her yesterday, and nothing came up except her Facebook page. Who is ungoogleable? How do you actually travel through life these days without leaving a footprint on the Internet? No Instagram page, she has never been interviewed, she's never participated in the Reykjavík marathon, she's never been involved in lawsuits. To be fair, there isn't much about me online, either.

My name wasn't mentioned in any of the articles about my father. I was a minor, and there are protections. They just said that he had left a wife and two children behind. I have a locked Instagram page (and one under a pseudonym, which I use for spying). I've never had a blog and I'm not on Bluesky. But I got the highest scores in the business department in my year. There was news about it on the university's website. You can look up my time in several races. There was an article in *Viðskiptablaðið* when I started my current job. With a picture and everything. And I'm on the list of employees on the website there. I exist. I am a real person. There is evidence of that.

But if Ásta Ólafardóttir didn't have a Facebook page, she would be completely invisible. A hidden woman.

"Have you been together long?"

"Yes, you could say that," she says. "We've been together since I was thirteen."

"Thirteen years old?" I can't hide my surprise.

She nods, looking half apologetic. "I know it's kind of crazy."

"And he's your age?"

I picture two cute kids, holding hands on the way home after school. My aunt was like that. She met her husband when she was fourteen. They're married and have two children now.

Ásta shrugs. "He was seventeen."

There must be such a look on my face because she hastens to add: "I know how it sounds. But it wasn't like that."

I don't know what she means by *that*. Does she mean he was held back at school? Or that they waited to have sex? For some reason that seems unlikely to me. Because I know how seventeen-year-old boys are. I mean, I was seventeen once.

"It always sounds gross when you do the math, I know. But I was a very mature thirteen year old. I had been taking care of myself for *years*, my mother was sick, and . . ." She pauses. Then hurries on. "Okay. So, he was disgustingly cool. I'll never forget it." One corner of her mouth lifts in a smile and her eyes go dreamy. "The first time we talked was outside the convenience store. It was freezing cold and dark—probably

January. And it was the kind of weather that can't decide if it's going to be snow or sleet. And I was way, way underdressed. He was standing there smoking. I don't know how he knew I was hungry or how he knew I had no money and that the fridge at home was empty. But he just looked at me, kind of up and down, and then went in and bought a hot dog and a chocolate milk for me. And I just fell in love. Being with him was nice. He even cooked for me. And I was never hungry again after I met him. He looked after me."

I am a very judgmental person. I know I am. And I'm trying not to be judgey now, but it's hard. This sounds like a child protection case, in more ways than one. With a little bit of rashness, I ask, "And what did your parents think of him being so much older?"

Ásta shrugs again. "Mom didn't even ask how old he was. But really, it's not like my mother and I ever talked much. She wasn't really in a position to look after anyone."

"And your dad?"

"We never had a relationship. I've only met him twice, I think. When I was little, he brought flowers for my mother and a doll for me. I don't even know his full name. I think he was married to someone else. But I still have the doll, you know? She's got this blue dress and has these red curls. I think maybe she was supposed to be a flamenco dancer."

"Is your mother sick?"

"She was. She said it was rheumatism. But in hindsight, I suspect maybe there was something else going on, too. Anyway, she was always completely impossible. Then she died when I was fifteen."

"From rheumatism?" I ask, surprised.

"No. Not that." Ásta clears her throat, looking down at the cats. "She hanged herself. In the shower."

I catch my breath. This is what I get for badgering people and snooping. Why am I digging when I know full well that I can't handle it when uncomfortable things are voiced? I *hate* situations like this. I never know what to say.

I feel like a complete ass, but I stammer, "Shit. Sorry, Ásta. God, I'm so sorry."

Ásta smiles sadly, as if to reassure me. "It's okay. It's been a long time."

"Tell me that you didn't . . . did you find her?" The question spills out of me before I can stop it.

Ásta looks at the sleeping kitten. She reaches out and strokes the tiny muzzle. This is too personal of a question. Way too personal. I'm about to apologize and say that of course she doesn't have to answer this, but then she says:

"I once read a book. About a woman who hanged herself in a bathroom. She knew her child was coming home from school, so she had written a note, which she stuck on the outside of the bathroom door. It said: 'Do not open. Call the police. I love you.'"

Ásta looks up at me. I swallow.

"But your mother?"

"Sometimes I wish she had at least locked the door. That she would have thought about how . . ." She pauses and then shakes her head. "Oh, not that it matters, not now."

"What did you do after your mother died?"

"I just moved in with Raggi. I told you he looked out for me."

I would like to ask what the child welfare authorities had said about the fact that a motherless, fifteen-year-old child moved in with a nineteen-year-old boy. But I know I've snooped enough tonight. And she owes me no explanation.

We sit in silence and listen to Io purring. I wonder if she is going to ask me about my parents and what I will say. But she doesn't. She picks up her phone and looks at the clock. "I have to go."

She leans forward, kisses Io between her ears, and this time I hear what she whispers: "Goodbye, my Io; please be sure to eat."

8

I don't have to type her name into the search bar. It appears below the box as soon as I open it, because she's the only one I look for on Instagram, at least on this account. I don't dare follow her, for obvious reasons, but I still make sure to never look at her page except when I'm logged in under my pseudonym. This is a fake account, and not a particularly well-faked one. I picked a common name at random, Sigga Guðmunds, googled "blond woman," and chose the first photo that came up to use as my profile picture. Because sometimes, I also watch her stories. And I know she can see who views them. Not that it should be a real concern—she has so many followers that "Sigga Guðmunds" must be just another face in a sea of faces. But this protects everyone.

I have no idea how many times a week I look at her Instagram. Possibly every day. Maybe more often sometimes, when he doesn't answer the phone, or when I don't hear from him for several days in a row, and I get this itch, this impatience that takes over all my thoughts and I just have to know what he's doing. Whether someone is visiting, whether they are on a trip, whether something happened, his parents-in-law died, whether one of their children was perhaps injured. She puts it all out there.

Sometimes he's a voice outside the picture, sometimes he's an arm pouring wine into a glass, sometimes he's smiling with a blond child in his arms, sometimes he's looking at the camera, at her, with those eyes he's promised are really mine. I tell myself it's better to see him there than not at all. But sometimes, when I lock the phone and put it down, and feel the loneliness closing in on me from all sides, I wonder if it is, in fact, much, much worse.

Experts are always warning people that what appears on social media is just a glossy, cooked-up version of reality. And it's amazing how good she is at smoothing over all the imperfections, ironing out her life, trimming it, setting it up so it seems perfect. She could be used as a textbook example of influencers lying on social media; if only people knew what I know. She seems to be living the perfect life, being the perfect mother, the perfect wife, the perfect woman.

But the truth is that the marriage is falling apart. It has been for years. She has no respect for Jói. She treats him like a meal ticket. He fell out of love with her years ago. But they have to think of the children. And I do think she is probably a decent mother, although if I were her I would think twice about how much she puts her children online. Maybe she sees them as a type of meal ticket, too.

I watch her stories. She's posted a lot today. I see the lunch her children brought to school this morning. The cup of coffee she drank once they were gone and she had the house to herself. There were fresh flowers on her desk when she sat down at the computer. She showed glimpses of the furniture she's designing. A beautiful chair. Then she shared some inspired advice from other influencers. The children came home. They went for a walk. There were beautiful autumn leaves on the trees. Then she cooked pasta. The sauce was, of course, made from scratch.

Her need for a perfect façade is sad, honestly. When Jói can finally be with me there will be no need for this shiny fake life, neatly packaged and on display. We don't need outside validation. Because we are the real thing.

Will she want to keep the house when he moves back here? Jói and I will have to find a place that is big enough to have rooms for the kids, too. I love this neighborhood, but I know everyone must make sacrifices. I envision us in a large, white, single-story house. It has an open floor plan, a big kitchen and enormous windows overlooking the ocean. I can take the kids on walks along the beach. We'll collect seashells, and if the weather is nice, we can take off our shoes and socks and play chicken with the waves. I have never been particularly good with children, but I am sure they will grow to like me. I can cook that pasta dish. It doesn't seem very complicated. I'm sure I can do it better than she can.

My phone vibrates in my palm and Jói's name is on the screen. He must have arrived at his hotel in New York.

9

It's Thursday night. And at one minute to nine there's a knock. I turn off the TV, a documentary about what new DNA technology tells us about the prehistoric people who lived in Scandinavia, get up, and open the door. Ásta stands outside. She is wearing the same blue coat, but has a soft white hat on her head that I haven't seen before.

There's snow on her shoulders and on her long eyelashes.

"Is it starting to snow?" I ask as I step aside to let her in.

"Barely," she says and takes off her coat. "Just a few flakes."

I look up at the sky. The lights from the city cast a yellow and pink glow on the low bank of clouds looming over the West side. A cold breeze creeps under my sweater and I quickly close the door.

"Did they have a good day?" asks Ásta, who is halfway into the bedroom.

"Yeah," I call after her.

I stop at the bedroom door, watching her greet Io and the kitten. Every time I see how much she cares for them, it warms me inside. And the affection seems mutual, because the purr in Io's chest increases by half when Ásta caresses her and scratches her and kisses her.

"Has she been eating?" Ásta sits on the floor next to my folded-up silk damask sheets, which have now become a cat bed.

"Mm-hm."

"Should I buy more cat food?"

"No, there's plenty. Do you want some tea?'

"Yes, please."

When I return with a cup in each hand, she is holding the kitten. She has lifted him up to her face and is gazing at him. His eyes are still closed; he sniffs the air and meeps.

"He's so beautiful," she says.

"I know," I say.

She kisses him on his tiny black nose and puts him back with Io.

I hand her the cup and sit on the bed. "How are you?"

"Good, thanks. Just a little tired."

I regard her more closely. She *looks* tired. Pale, with circles under the eyes. "Oh? A lot to do?"

"Always *so* much. And also, I am not sleeping well. I dream a lot—some ridiculous dreams, complete nonsense. Then I wake up exhausted, as if I've been up all night."

"Have you tried taking melatonin? You can get it at a pharmacy without a prescription."

"Maybe I will."

My phone beeps. I take it out of my pocket. There's a message from Jói.

Good night, my sweet one.

Good night to you, too, I write.

When I put the phone down and look up, I realize that I must have smiled involuntarily, because there's a grin on Ásta's face.

"Your boyfriend?" she asks.

I nod.

"So you don't live together? Is this a new thing?"

I sip my tea, wondering how much I can tell her. She opened up to me on Tuesday. It would be rude if I didn't reciprocate, right? And I rarely get the chance to talk about Jói. It should be safe to do that with her. There's no way that they move in the same circles and she would know who he is.

"He lives in Cologne. He's a pilot."

"Oh ho!" she says. "Long distance relationship?"

I nod. "But he's moving back to Iceland soon. He's just waiting for the right time."

"The right time for what?"

"When Icelandair starts hiring," I say.

"Ah, okay, like that. God, don't you find it hard to be so far apart? I was going completely crazy being here in Reykjavík when Raggi was back East. It's not that I'm not used to being alone, because, I mean, he's always been at sea. And he's sometimes away for weeks. Which, honestly, is probably why I'm always reading. It's just that when he was at sea, I knew where he was and what he was doing and with whom. But when I was here and he was back East . . . I sometimes imagined the worst."

"What's the worst?" I ask.

"That he's with someone else."

I clear my throat.

"Long distance works well for me." I say, before diving into the well-rehearsed speech I give myself on bad days. "I have my own space, he has his. I don't really need someone in my business all the time, you know. Plus, I have a lot to do at work these days. There's a chance that I might be promoted to Marketing Manager. It's a big deal. And this really is the best of both worlds. We don't have to argue about who takes out the trash. It keeps us from getting lost in the mundane. It maintains excitement in the relationship."

Ásta wrinkles her forehead. "But is he ever going to move here? I mean, excitement can't be maintained forever. At some point, you want someone to share the mundane stuff with, right? Isn't that the whole point?"

"Sure, of course. But right now, right now . . . I like being independent. Self-sufficient. I need my freedom."

"To do what?"

"Huh?" I say.

"Freedom to do what?"

I stare at her. I feel myself starting to blush. "I just need my own space. My own . . . haven of sorts, you know." Then I turn from defense into attack. "I don't need a man to complete my life. I have a very fun and fulfilling life."

"Yes," she says apologetically. "Sorry. Of course. I didn't mean it that way. Don't get me wrong. But . . . don't you ever get lonely? I got Io as soon as I moved South. It probably sounds pathetic, but I really can't sleep alone."

I snort. "Why would I be lonely? I like living alone. And I sleep much better when there isn't someone snoring next to me and stealing the covers."

Ásta smiles. She's so ridiculously beautiful. I wonder if she's aware of that. She doesn't act like she knows. "I wish I was like you."

I smile, too. The compliment warms me, even though I may not have painted a completely honest picture of my life for her. But I've said this so many times to myself that I've almost started to believe it. And some days it's absolutely true.

"I mean, we talk a lot," I say. "I know exactly what's going on in his life. We cheer each other on. I just don't need to know where he is all the time."

"But you must visit him sometimes? Or him you? I mean, you must meet?"

"Yes, of course. Often. I regularly fly out and meet him in all sorts of exciting places. We recently spent two nights in Rome. And we're going to meet in Boston in a few weeks. Naturally, he travels a lot for work."

"But you never go to his house?"

"No. It's more fun this way."

Ásta stares at me, her blue eyes wide with horror. "Got it," she says. "Right."

"Not all relationships have to be the same."

"Of course not," she says. "So . . . how did you two meet?"

"We'd known each other for a long time," I say. "Before we started dating."

My tone is short because I don't want to talk more about Jói. It's no business of hers how I conduct my life or how our relationship is. It doesn't concern anyone but me and Jói. But it's as if she didn't realize that I've had enough of her prying, because she seems ready to keep asking.

I've opened my mouth to change the subject when there is a knock on the front door.

She looks at me, terrified. "Are you expecting someone?"

"No." I'm startled by the look on her face. Like a kid caught doing something illicit.

"It's probably just someone selling something. Kids collecting cans for a school drive. I swear they come, like, twice a month." I put my cup of tea down and stand.

Ásta remains on the floor, and I feel her big eyes following me out of the room.

I open the front door. Outside stands a man. He is dark-haired, with a dark beard and brown eyes. He is tall, broad shouldered, and wearing a black coat.

"Good evening," he says.

"Good evening," I say.

"Is Ásta here?"

I hear a rustle behind me and his eyes flick over my shoulder. I turn my head. Ásta stands between the kitchen and the living room. Her face is pale; her big eyes stare at the man.

"Raggi," she whispers.

"Hey, baby," he says. But he's not looking at her. His eyes scan the kitchen, the living room, the hall. He takes in my coffee machine, the sofa in the living room, my shoes, my coat, the letters lying on top of the radiator in the hall.

He looks at me.

"How are you," he says. "My name is Ragnar Stefánsson. Nice to meet you."

He smiles, but the smile does not reach his eyes. He gives me his hand.

I don't want to touch it. But it hangs between us, right in front of me, as insistent as a question. I want to knock his hand away, tell him to leave. But that's not what you do. That would be rude. So I shake his hand.

His palm is big; he takes mine and squeezes so hard that it hurts.

Io walks into the living room.

When she sees Ragnar, she freezes. She stares at him, and I see the hair on her back rise and her tail grow as big as a wash brush.

"Well," says Ragnar and looks at Ásta in surprise. "So, she's here then?"

"Yes," says Ásta. "Here she is. I'll get my coat."

"Oh, are we going?" asks Ragnar.

"Yes," says Ásta. "We're leaving."

10

I worry about Ásta all Friday. I can't explain why, and honestly, it's not like me at all. I've always avoided getting tangled up in other people's messes. They do not concern me. But I realize with surprise that I care about Ásta.

There was nothing this Ragnar said or did that suggests an actual problem. But I can't stop thinking about the look of terror on her face when he knocked. The fear in her eyes when she asked if I was expecting someone. The look on her face when she came forward and saw him standing next to me is etched in my mind.

But she's always spoken well of him. More than once, she's said that he saved her. That she can't imagine living alone. How hard it was to be apart. I must have misunderstood something. I must be reading this all wrong. Maybe there was a terrible event they don't want me involved in. Maybe some crisis, someone sick, some uncertainty. And he's told her he'll come get her if things go wrong? Of course, they don't owe me an explanation.

As I cook myself an elaborate dinner, I can't stop thinking about her. While I rub marinade into my raw steak, the bloody juices soaking my fingers, I wonder if things are okay. As I chop broccoli I wonder if he has done something to her. Because I also remember how Io froze when she saw him. How she arched her back and how her tail puffed out. When they were gone, I went into the room to check on Io, and she had already moved the kitten. It took me a long time, but I finally found them inside my wardrobe. There they were in the corner, deep inside, under my long dresses, as far from the front door as you could possibly get.

I decided it was best to leave them be. When I woke up this morning, they were back in place, on top of my sheets in the corner.

As I chew the tender meat I realize that I want to call Ásta. But she asked me not to call and to text her instead. Why did she ask that? Because of him? But what should I say? Ask how she is? Whether she is totally safe and healthy? I consider making something up, like there's a need for cat litter or more of the special food for nursing mothers. But she would know that I was lying. She brought cat litter yesterday and only about a third of the food is gone.

I eat the last bit of meat on my plate. I chew it in silence. I sit for a while, looking out the window. Then I go into the kitchen to clean up.

11

I sleep badly that night. Waking up way too early, a quarter to seven, and knowing as soon as I open my eyes that there's no way I'll be able to fall back asleep. It's four hours until she arrives. *Or until she had planned to come*, whispers that small voice somewhere in the back of my mind, where my darker thoughts reside.

Jói will never leave his wife.

Þovard will never promote me.

There's black mold in my walls.

Despite all my hard work no one will ever truly respect me.

I'll get that cancer women get because they didn't have children and then I'll die alone before I turn forty and leave nothing behind, as if I wasn't even here.

If I walk into the ocean, scavenging sea creatures will dismember my body in two weeks and then my bones will sink to the ocean floor.

I silence the voice. I am well practiced at that.

I go out for a run, like I always do on Saturdays. The city has frozen over during the night. A glittering frost covers everything. It stars the asphalt beneath my feet, while branches and grass refract the rays of the morning sun like crystals.

I shower when I get home, feed Io, pour myself a coffee, and have a healthy smoothie. It is twenty minutes past nine. I always clean on Saturdays. I start in the kitchen, then the bathroom, and then I vacuum the living room. I don't want to wake up Io, so I leave the bedroom alone. It's half past ten. I decide it's time to clean out the fridge.

It is ten minutes past eleven. The refrigerator is clean, but Ásta is not here.

I go to the living room, look out the window, west along Ránargata in the direction of Framnesvegur, where she lives. But, of course, she could come from some other direction. Maybe she went to yoga first, or the gym or something.

I sit on the sofa. Pick up the phone, open Instagram, and scroll, without taking anything in. It's seventeen past the hour.

There's a knock. I jump up from the sofa, run down the hall, and open the door.

I am indescribably relieved when I see Ásta outside. She has no bruises, no limbs in casts. She looks like herself, although she is pale and has dark circles under her eyes. Does she still sleep badly?

"Hi," I say, a little too loudly, and let her in.

"Hi." She smiles tiredly, takes off her coat, and then walks into the bedroom. I follow her, like an anxious young mother. She's stiff as she bends down, and her face twitches in pain as she sits on the floor.

"Are you okay?" I ask.

She doesn't seem to hear me. Or maybe she's ignoring me. Io rolls onto her back when Ásta pats her. She scratches her belly, then picks up the kitten and brings it up to her face. She closes her eyes and buries her nose in the black fur. Then she presses him to her cheek and bows her head. It's like a painting of the Virgin Mary that I once saw in a museum. All that's missing is the halo.

"Are you okay?" I ask again.

She opens her eyes, looking at me. "Did you say something?"

"I was asking if you were okay?"

She smiles faintly. "Yes. All fine. Except, I'm just—oh, this is so stupid. But I've lost hearing in my right ear. Just temporarily. I went swimming and got water in my ear, or a wax blockage or something. So I just can't hear a thing on this side." She points to her right shoulder.

"Have you had it checked?" I ask, raising my voice.

"Nope. I'm sure it's nothing. It'll get better in a few days."

"Are you sure? There's a health center just the next street over. It's actually closed right now since it's Saturday, but I can definitely take you to a doctor's office if you want."

She shakes her head. "That's so sweet. But, no, it's all right. It's probably just stress. It's crazy right now. I have to submit a proposal for my final project next week. But if my ear's not better after that, maybe I'll have it looked at. But how are you?"

"Just fine."

"Your apartment is so clean. Were you tidying?"

"Yeah. Saturdays are my cleaning day," I say. "Nothing like laundry to make it a *sadder day.*"

Ásta kisses the kitten on the muzzle and puts him back with Io. He immediately goes looking for a nipple. Maybe she didn't hear me. But the joke was too bad to bear repeating.

"I wanted to apologize for last time," says Ásta. "About Raggi. How he just showed up."

I cross my arms. "No problem." And then I ask her the thing that's been bothering me. "So . . . he didn't know Io was here? He seemed really surprised to see her."

"No." Ásta licks her lips. "Not really."

"Why?"

"Oh." She pauses for a moment. "I just thought it was simpler, you know?"

"No," I say. "Not so much."

She extends a slender index finger, takes it with her other hand, and begins to poke at the skin around the nail. "He, Raggi is sometimes just . . . a bit . . . and I thought maybe he would be hurt if . . . if . . . Io had gone somewhere else. Like she's . . . rejecting him, you know?"

"I didn't think he was particularly fond of her."

"Raggi is . . . he's afraid that people will leave him. Maybe it's because his dad, he left. When Raggi was just little. He experienced a lot of rejection. He's sensitive."

"Yeah, okay."

The little voice in the back of my mind stirs, whispering something about what my father's disappearance might have done to me. But I push it down. It is not something I ever like to think about. Then I frown. Because what Ásta just said raises another, worse question.

"But . . . Ásta, if he didn't know the cat was here, how did he know you were here?"

Ásta laughs. But the laughter is low and mirthless. "Oh. It turns out he installed some sort of app on my phone. So he can see where it is. Kind of like 'find my phone,' you know?"

I stare at her. "He put that on your phone without telling you?"

She shakes her head. "It's not like that. He just forgot to tell me. It's just to help you find your phone if it's stolen, or if you lose it. I'm always losing phones! I'm so obnoxiously forgetful it's not funny. Raggi always helps me with all the updates and such on the phone. I'm totally hopeless with gadgets."

"And did he put an app on his phone so you can see where he is?"

She shakes her head. "No."

"Ásta . . ."

"Or yes! Maybe he did. Probably! See? I was just saying that I don't know anything about this phone; I hardly go online with it."

"So if he goes on his phone now he can see where you are? All the time?"

"Yes."

I hesitate. I try to say what I have to say carefully. "Ásta, I don't think that sounds quite right."

Now she's the one snorting. And there's a challenge in her gaze. "Let it go, Unnur. And would you *please* stop making this sound all suspicious, like it's something shady. Raggi is a good man. And he loves me. That's what matters."

"But, Ásta," I say gently. "Shouldn't love be based on trust? You shouldn't have to keep the other person on a leash."

"Really?" she says dryly. "So it's better to be with someone you never see? I don't think that sounds very reassuring."

My voice turns defensive. "We're not talking about me."

"Raggi is only looking out for me, the way he has ever since we met. He just wants to be involved in my life and participate. It's not like he's somewhere abroad doing god knows what with god knows who. I'm sorry, I don't think you can judge me and my relationship when you haven't even been to your boyfriend's home."

Ásta has turned red in the face. I have, too.

We stare at each other. It feels like if I break eye contact first, it will somehow mean that I've lost.

Ásta is the first to look away. But I get no sense of victory. Instead, an unpleasant feeling spreads in my stomach. The conversation wasn't supposed to go like this.

"I have to go," says Ásta.

I don't say anything. Just watch her kiss the cats and get up. She moans again, as if she hurts somewhere. But I don't ask her about it.

12

Jói was my brother's friend. *Is* my brother's friend. I have vague memories of him from when I was starting middle school and they were finishing high school. Grown men, I thought.

He came back to Iceland when my brother got married. And there I was standing at the bar during the reception, trying to order a gin and tonic. But the bartender didn't see me, no matter how much I waved. He served everyone else.

I had felt invisible for a long time. I had worked hard in college, more focused on getting good grades than making friends. It had been a mistake. I miscalculated how much of this country is based on relationships. Who you know matters more than anything. No one bothers to ask what your transcript looks like if you have a friend recommending you for the job.

So there I was, fresh out of college, working a crappy job, surrounded by idiots who didn't know anything, seriously thinking about giving it all up, applying to some fancy foreign school—where people are valued, not by lineage or by the district in which they were born—never mind if I had to pay the student loans for the rest of my life.

I kept trying to wave the bartender over. He continued to ignore me. I wondered if anyone would notice if I disappeared completely. Whether anyone would miss me.

I sighed and looked to the side. And there he was, looking straight at me. He wasn't exactly smiling, not with his lips, but there was a twinkle in his eyes. And suddenly I felt like the world around us dissolved. That it wasn't me but the world that was disappearing. He *saw me.*

I remembered him, but he didn't recognize me. The little kid.

We left the reception early that night. My brother had gotten married on a Friday, and Jói and I spent the whole rest of the weekend together, the two of us alone in the world. But then reality finally kicked in, as it always does. He told me how things were. I was shocked, but then I made a decision. Because I couldn't let go of him. He was a good man, and good things take time. Rome wasn't built in a day, as they say. And I've always known how to be patient.

I know what people think. That of course I should know better. But we are not a cliché.

Jói is a responsible man in a difficult situation. He can't leave his family just like that. His wife is still getting her business going. She supported him financially when he was studying. They decided that then it would be her turn. And the children must be given time to be children.

It's just a difficult situation. For all concerned. The care he has for his kids and even his wife, despite having fallen out of love with her, makes me want him even more. He puts others above himself.

Good things happen slowly. But that doesn't mean they don't happen at all.

13

There is a man standing on my porch when I come home from work. I stop on the sidewalk outside of my house and stare up at him. A chill runs down my spine, like a bad omen. This is Ragnar.

"Where's Ásta?" I ask. "Is she okay?"

Ragnar has been leaning against the railing while waiting for me, relaxed. He smiles. "Hello," he says with emphasis, as if he's trying to teach me some manners. "Ásta is at work, cleaning the kindergarten. She's fine. You don't have to worry. I just wanted to talk to you."

I go up the stairs. He backs up a bit, giving me space to get to the door.

"About what?"

"Can I come in? Have a cup of coffee? I wanted to talk to you."

"About?"

"The cats."

"Did Ásta ask you to come?"

"It won't take long, I promise."

I study him. He's still smiling. He has beautiful teeth and twinkling brown eyes. This is hardly the same man who appeared at my house on Thursday night. Maybe I really have been misunderstanding it all.

I take the key out of my coat pocket and open the door. "Milk or sugar?"

"Just black, please."

I tell him to have a seat while I make the coffee.

When I walk into the living room with a cup of coffee in each hand, he's man-spreading in the middle of the sofa, sitting happily with his arms out to either side along the back, as if he's trying to take up as much space as he can. I hand him the cup and sit in the armchair farthest from him.

He takes a sip of his coffee, then raises an eyebrow and hums. "Good coffee. A nice coffeemaker. Expensive?"

I ignore the question. "You said you wanted to talk about the cats?"

He straightens. "I was going to offer to take them. You probably have plenty of other things to do instead of looking after them. I can tell you're a busy lady." He points to the suit I'm wearing. It is bottle green and suits me well, if I do say so myself. "You have a good job, you have to work in the mornings and on weekends and go to cocktail parties and out to eat with clients. You don't have time to take care of pets."

I frown. Of course, he is absolutely right. But a whisper tells me not to trust him. It's the little voice at the back of my mind. The one I'm so good at silencing.

"Did Ásta send you? Does she know you're here?"

He sighs, looking at me, his expression sincere, as if he is about to confide a secret. "Ásta is in no condition to take care of these cats. You know what I mean? I don't want to speak out of turn here, but Ásta . . . She's so sensitive. She just can't handle it. She was a wreck when that bitch ran away. She cried for two days straight."

I frown.

I don't like him describing Io as a bitch. Granted, I haven't known the cat for very long, but we met at what turned out to be a very challenging time in her life.

And Io takes good care of her kitten. She's a good mom, she never pees inside, doesn't scratch my furniture, and she barely sheds. She's a model cat, I think, although I don't know many and have little comparison. Io tries her best—and can you really ask for more?

"Any sane person can see that it's not normal," continues Ragnar. "Ásta needs to focus on school. She needs to stop this."

"This what?"

"The business with the cats. It's causing her a lot of anxiety."

I stare at him. He looks back at me, his dark eyes full of concern, for Ásta, I assume.

"Does it bother you that she's coming here?" I ask.

Ragnar sighs and shakes his head. Like I disappointed him with this question. "You know, I didn't really want to say anything because I always feel like I'm . . . kind of going behind her back when I talk about it." He pauses, as if debating whether to continue. I involuntarily squirm forward in my seat. "Ásta is very sick. Now, mental illness is nothing to be ashamed of, but she still has to deal with it. She needs help, from professionals. I've tried talking to her, but she doesn't want people to know . . ."

"Mental illness?" I interject.

He sighs again, heavily, as if all the trials of the world rest on his shoulders. "She's not well. Yesterday, I found her out on the rocks at Seltjarnarnes. She had climbed down to the beach, except it's no beach, it's just rocks, huge boulders. Really dangerous when they're wet, too. I don't know what she was going to do, if she was trying to . . ."

He leaves it up to me to fill in the blank. I cover my mouth.

"She had her shoes off and her feet were bloody and her face was all scratched from the rocks when I found her. It was just lucky she had her phone with her, otherwise I never would have known where she was."

I'm really upset. "Are you telling the truth?"

He nods. "It's a lot of work to take care of her. But I do it because I love her. That's why I think it would be a great relief—for everyone—if these cats weren't in the picture."

I stare at him. I can't make up my mind about whether I believe him or not. I know mental illness is often invisible, but this description of Ásta doesn't match what I've seen. Maybe she has a little self-doubt, is insecure, but not like she's on the verge of suicide. She doesn't seem like the type to hurt herself. On the contrary, she seems like a person who has considerable self-reliance. She found her mother hanging in the bath when she was fifteen years old; she has no family to speak of but is finishing her degree in literature. I don't know if I would have done as well in her shoes. But what experience do I have with self-harm and mental illness? I don't know anyone who deals with either, as far as I'm aware. And how often have I met her? Five times? It's not like I know her.

I must have been silent for too long, because Ragnar clears his throat.

"Wouldn't I be doing you a favor, too?" he asks. "Ásta told me that you didn't want the cats. They've got to bother you."

There's a different note in his voice. More determined. I don't like it.

"What are you going to do with them?" I ask suspiciously. "Take them to the shelter?"

"Does it matter? Do you really care? It's not like you want these cats here. Scratching your fine furniture and peeing in the corners."

His tone is impatient now, even bordering on hostile. I become even more suspicious.

"Are you going to have them put down?"

He laughs. “Do you have any idea how much it costs to euthanize cats?”

I put the coffee cup down. Stand. “I want you to leave.”

Ragnar stands, too. Looks around. “Where are they?”

He goes into my bedroom. I run after him, but he’s faster. He takes three steps and stops at the door.

Io is lying on her side on the blanket looking up at him. The kitten is nursing. Ragnar enters. Io hisses. He pretends not to hear her, and then he bends down, pulls the kitten off the teat, and picks him up.

“No,” I say, too late.

The kitten cries, distressed about being ripped away from his mother.

Ragnar studies him. There is a look of disdain on his face. Ice floods my veins.

“Wow, he’s tiny. And he hasn’t even opened his eyes yet.”

Io stands up. She meows emphatically.

“Put him down,” I say. “She doesn’t like people holding him.”

But Ragnar acts like he doesn’t hear me. He stares at the kitten, who twists and mews at the air.

“I’ve never understood the fascination with cats. Why have them? They just use people. Live at someone’s house, eat their food, get petted. So they can just take off whenever it suits them." He looks at me. "You know what acts like that? A parasite."

Io yowls again; she jumps onto the bed, staring at the kitten, who is still crying. Io's meows are drawn out and pleading. It's obvious what she wants. She is asking Ragnar to return the kitten.

Ragnar looks at Io with contempt. "This cat has always hated me. But you don't, little kitten, do you? You don't know anything. You can't even see."

He raises the kitten to his face to see him better. Then he looks at me and grins.

"Damn, he's so small. Look at those paws. These little bones . . . they must be very fragile. And that tiny head. I could crush it. I could probably do it with one hand." His palm rests lightly on the kitten's head, but his words sit heavy in my stomach. "I probably wouldn't have to squeeze very hard."

I hold out my hand. "Let me have the kitten. Give him to me and get out of here."

I'm trying to sound determined, but I can hear my voice shaking.

Ragnar looks at me, time stretching, as if we are approaching a black hole.

Then he starts laughing. But even though his face is split into a smile, there's no joy on it. He hands me the kitten. I grab the little guy with both hands, holding him against my chest. Ragnar steps closer. He is right next to me, towering, so I have to tilt my head to look up at him. I back up, but only get one step and then I'm against the wall.

"You bloody snob," Ragnar hisses. "Think you're better than us, don't you? Didn't anyone teach you how to take a joke?"

He turns around and walks out.

"Thanks for the coffee!" he calls. Then I hear the front door slam.

I slide down the wall. Io jumps to the floor and wiggles into my arms. She sniffs the kitten and then begins to lick him up and down, as if to remove all traces of Ragnar. I stroke her soft, shiny back.

"Hey there, sweet Io," I say. "It's all right. Your baby is fine. We're fine."

But that's not true. My palms are numb, my mouth is dry, and my heart is pounding in my chest. When I recover a bit, I run a hot bath, hoping that the feeling of helplessness Ragnar left behind will wash away. But it's still there when I go to sleep, like when someone touches you uninvited and the unpleasant sensation of their hand lingers on your skin for hours, like a tingling, invisible bruise.

14

The next day I call Jói. Tell him everything. Fortunately, my timing is good. He was coming from the gym and is on his way home, but has time to talk.

"Poor girl," he says.

"I know," I say. "It's miserable."

"And she doesn't want any help from professionals?"

I gape. I'm so taken aback by the question that I am speechless for a moment.

"You believe him?" I ask when I get my voice back.

The question seems to surprise him. "Why would he lie?"

I gasp. "Why?! Why was he here trying to take the cats? That's what I want to know!"

"Calm down," says Jói, in an unbearably paternal tone. "Because cats are trouble, I hear. You were saying that yourself just the day before yesterday."

"Yeah, but . . . but . . . that doesn't mean it's okay. Do you know how much she loves these cats? And don't you tell me to calm down, Jói. You didn't see him; you didn't see how he changed the moment he realized his nice guy act wasn't working on me. It was like he stopped trying, dropped the mask. And when he picked up the kitten and started talking about how small and fragile he was. It was a threat."

I can literally hear him furrow his brow, frowning. "Why do you say that? I mean, I've heard you talk about how small this kitten is, how fragile it is, as if it's not fully developed and was born way too early. Are you sure you didn't just misunderstand the guy?"

I close my eyes and see Ragnar's expression again as he stood over me, way too close. I can feel my back against the wall as I realized there was nowhere to escape.

How can I explain this to him? Can I get him to see? Jói is forty-two years old. Eldest of three brothers. He is 195 centimeters tall. Broad shoulders, goes to the gym three times a week. How long has it been since someone threatened him? And if he was threatened now, he might not even notice. Because who would intimidate him? I think about his wife. What would Jói say to her if she told him she felt afraid of a man who came into their home? The small voice at the back of my mind whispers that I might not like the answer to that question, so I push it down.

"It was a threat," I say. "Trust me."

"Okay." He sighs. "I believe you. If you say so."

But his tone says that he doesn't.

"Okay," he says again. "I really have to go to . . ."

"Sure," I say. "No problem."

"Talk to you later?"

"Sounds good."

I hang up. I sit on the sofa for a long time and bite my nails. Had I been reading Ásta wrong this whole time? Could it be that Ragnar was telling the truth and I'm just misunderstanding it all?

I bite the nail on my thumb down to the quick. I watch the blood pool at the edge, becoming a shiny deep red drop that sticks out like a precious stone. I stand up before it slides off my finger and onto the white couch. Because it would be completely impossible to get blood out of it.

15

It's Tuesday. After work, I go for a long run. When I get home, I take a bath, then boil pasta, pour pesto over it from a jar, and eat it sitting in front of the TV. I like to cook—Jói and I eat so much good food when we're traveling, and I love being able to test out recipes myself once I'm home again—but tonight I'm just not up for it.

Io jumps onto the couch with me and asks for scritches. She's just started doing this, daring to leave the kitten alone for a while. The first few days she only left him to eat, drink, and go to the litter box. She's clearly starting to trust him to be on his own for a few minutes. Or maybe she's starting to trust me?

I stroke her back, scratch her first behind one ear and then the other. She purrs in capital letters and closes her eyes again. She lifts her chin. I've learned that means she wants to have her neck scratched. I do as I am asked.

There is a knock on the front door. Io opens her eyes and looks at me.

"Come on," I say, standing up. Io jumps off the sofa and follows me into the hall, tail tall.

I open the door.

Ásta stands outside.

I catch my breath. One of her cheeks is blue and bruised.

"What happened?" I ask. "Was it Ragnar?"

"No," she says. "I just fell. I'm fine."

I don't know if I believe her. I think of the rocky beach Ragnar said he found her on, all cut up. But either way, I can't just leave her standing out there in the cold. "Come in."

She takes off her coat, and when she takes off her hat, I see that her forehead is bruised as well. But the bruise there is green and yellow. I don't know if that means it's older or if it's because the skin is thinner there.

"How did you fall?" I ask. We don't know each other well, but we've had surprisingly deep conversations every time she's been over. I am hoping that means she would tell me if something was wrong.

"I was just being clumsy," she says, and my heart sinks a little bit in my chest. "Oh, hello, my Io!"

She bends down to the cat, who has been loitering at her feet since she entered. She winds around Ásta's ankles, clearly thrilled to see her.

Ásta takes her in her arms and walks into the bedroom. "Wow, the kitten has grown!"

"I know," I say as I follow her. "Can I offer you anything? Coffee? Tea? Water?"

"No, thanks," she says with a smile.

She's lost weight. I can see it.

"Are you hungry?" I ask. "I have leftover pasta from earlier."

"No. Thanks anyway. I've been a bit listless and weird. I thought maybe I was getting a stomach bug, I felt so sick, but then I didn't vomit at all."

I sit on the bed, cross my legs like I'm getting ready to meditate.

My phone rings in the living room. It's probably Jói.

"You're not going to answer?" she asks.

"No," I say.

"Why not?"

"Whatever it is, it can wait."

"Maybe it's your boyfriend?"

"Could be."

"He's married, isn't he?" She looks at me with those blue eyes.

For a moment I think about lying to her. But I want her to trust me. Doesn't that mean I have to trust her, too?

"Yeah."

She nods. But there's no pity in her expression. No judgment. She just nods. "Does he call often?"

"When he can. It's not a problem when he's flying, but harder when he's at home. Then it can be challenging."

"What does he tell his wife?"

"I don't know. I don't ask."

"Because you don't want to know?"

"I guess."

"You never talk about her?"

I take a deep breath. My shoulders slump. "First, he told me everything. How she treats him. The way she talks to him. She doesn't appreciate him. She doesn't realize what a treasure she has. She's ungrateful. He's stuck. She's been at home with the kids, so if he leaves her, she'll definitely get custody of the children. The marriage is over. It has been for a long time. They don't even sleep together."

"He tells you that?"

"Yes."

"And you believe him?" Again, there is no judgment in her voice. This is just a question.

"Yes."

"And now you never talk about her?"

"No."

She nods thoughtfully. "Have you heard of Planet Nine?"

I frown, then shake my head. "Planet Nine? What are you talking about?" Is the head injury making her confused?

"Okay, you know how there are eight planets in the solar system, right?"

I wonder if I should point out to her that there is actually still some debate about whether Pluto should count as a planet. I just listened to a podcast about this recently and I could explain why. But seeing the earnest look on her beautiful face I decide this is probably neither the time nor the place to dive into the finer points of astronomy, so I just nod, signaling that I did indeed know that.

"There are theories that there is an unknown, hidden planet in the solar system. There are scientists who say it's huge and has such a large orbit around the sun that it only passes the Earth every thousand million years."

"Okay," I say hesitantly, not quite sure where she's going with this or why this wasn't mentioned on the podcast.

"So we never see the planet. But still its gravitational forces work on us every single day."

"I didn't know that." I don't know if I quite believe it either, but her lovely face is lit up and animated, telling me about this secret planet, so I just nod.

"And some scientists think it was followed by a meteor shower the last time it passed the earth. And that's what killed the dinosaurs."

"Yeah, okay. And what happens when it comes back?"

Ásta shrugs. "I guess everything goes to hell."

I laugh. Ásta smiles.

Out front, something rustles. Bangs. Then big heavy steps.

Ragnar walks through my door.

His hair is disheveled, his black coat is open, and his eyes are burning with anger.

Beside me, I see Ásta huddle into herself. She makes a little sound, like a whimper. I jump to my feet, hands outstretched, to push him back out. But he straightens his arm. An arm longer than mine. He shoves hard on my chest. I fall back onto the bed, legs in the air.

He bends down, yanks Ásta up by the hair.

She screams. I scream. But it's like he doesn't hear us. He doesn't even look at me. His face is completely expressionless. He turns and walks into the living room, with Ásta in tow. She halfcrawls after him, stumbles, screams again, tries to get to her feet, but slips. I try to sit up, but it's like my body is paralyzed. I hear them moving, hear something banging against the doorframe between the living room and the kitchen.

Then the front door slams, and cold silence falls over the apartment like a shroud.

16

My fingers are shaking so much it takes me three tries to dial 112. They're still shaking when the police arrive a little later. They make me go over everything twice.

"Then the door just slammed and I didn't hear anything else."

I'm standing with two police officers in my foyer. A man and a woman. They're not particularly tall, but somehow they fill the space as if the entryway has shrunk in half. Maybe because they're both wearing vests with all kinds of pockets. For a moment, an insatiable curiosity to know what's in them washes over me. Nail clippers? Duct tape? Condoms? Are they really ready for anything?

There are literally no traces of the incident, other than strands of Ásta's blond hair on the kitchen floor and her old, worn-out sneakers still by the door. Otherwise, there is no indication of what happened. About the monster that broke in on us.

The policewoman's phone rings. She answers. I hear a woman's voice on the other line, but I can't make out the words. They had told me that another car had gone to Framnesvegur, to the home of Ásta and Ragnar. Is this about them?

The policewoman looks at me. And for a moment I fear the worst. That he murdered her. Threw her off the pier. Or dumped her body in a fissure in a lava field. My stomach clenches with dread. But then the policewoman frowns and sighs.

"Thanks," she says and hangs up.

"What? Is she okay?"

The policewoman inhales loudly through her nose. "Yes. They are at home. Just watching TV. Say everything's fine."

I stare at her. I can hardly believe my ears. "Everything's *fine*? Did he say that or did she?"

"Both," says the policewoman.

"Didn't they see the bruises she had?"

"She says she fell."

"But . . . but he pulled her out by the hair. Right in front of me. Her shoes are still here. He pulled her out by the hair, in her socks. Who voluntarily goes out and leaves their shoes?"

I point to the sneakers, the only evidence I have.

"She says they went home together, that it was a joint decision. She was here and he picked her up."

"She's lying," I say. "She's lying!"

The policewoman sighs. "These are difficult cases. She has to want to leave."

I stare at her. The woman's eyes are full of compassion, and I can't help but wonder how many times she's been in a similar situation.

"You were right to call. Thank you."

"But . . ."

The walkie-talkie that the man has on his chest crackles. Unintelligible speech comes from it. But the officers clearly understand, because they look at each other, then at me, and the woman says, "We have to go. But feel free to call back if . . . if anything else happens, okay?"

I nod.

Then they both say goodbye, walk out the door, and close it behind them.

17

I try to call Ásta as soon as the police have left. She doesn't answer, so I call again and again. When I try to call the fourth time, the phone has been switched off. I text a message. I know she probably won't see it right away, but she will someday.

Ásta, I can help you. You can always come to me. We can go to the police together or to the Women's Shelter or to the Stígamót Foundation Against Sexual Violence. Or we don't have to go anywhere and you can just stay here.

I read it over. Is he monitoring her messages? Will this talk of police and the women's shelter get her into more trouble?

I'm not sure, so I delete it, and write instead:

Ásta, you are always welcome here. You know that.

I hit SEND.

The night passes with no response. The next day and night follow without a text or acknowledgment of any kind.

I google "how to help a person in an abusive relationship." Most of what I read matches what the police said: If the person doesn't decide to leave on their own, there's little that can be done, other than letting them know that you're there when they decide to run away. I also read that abusive relationships are life threatening. Of course I know that. Men are always killing women. But I also learn that the most dangerous time in an abusive relationship is when the woman tries to leave.

I can't concentrate at work. The thought of her there with him is unbearable. I text her again. Change tactics.

Ásta, Io misses you so terribly. Whenever she hears traffic, she jumps to her feet, tail in the air, and runs purring to the front door, hoping it's you. And when you don't come, her tail drops. Ásta, she's so sad. Why don't you come visit her? And the kitten. He has grown so much! I think he'll open his eyes soon. Don't you want him to see you?

I read the message twice after I send it. Decide to add:

Also Io's food is completely finished now. You know, that special food for nursing mothers? I don't know where to get it. You'll need to get more and drop by with it.

Another whole day goes by without her answering. I think about camping out in front of her job, but then realize I never asked which preschool she works at. There are a few of them in the neighborhood, but she might well be cleaning in Grafarvogur or Mosfellsbær for all I know.

I go home, cook an omelette that I don't eat. I sit in front of the TV, but I've been there for only a few minutes when I get up.

I can't stop thinking about her screams as he pulled her out by her hair. The bang I heard against the doorframe between the living room and kitchen. What hit it? Her head?

I put on a coat and shoes and set off west, in the direction of Framnesvegur.

Neither of them are in the phone book. I had to look up Ásta in the National Register to find her address. It turns out to be a basement apartment. The entry is behind the house, through the garden.

The door is made of weathered wood in dire need of varnishing. On it is a small diamond-shaped window, where someone has hung a little sign that says *Ásta and Ragnar*, in fine writing.

Ásta has written this.

I clench my knuckles and knock hard.

After a while I hear footsteps. I see movement through the window and then the door opens. Ragnar stands guard.

He stares at me and does not hide the contempt in his face. "What are you doing here?"

"I'm here to talk to Ásta. Is she home?"

"None of your business."

"I'm going to talk to her," I say firmly. "I've been trying to reach her."

"She doesn't want to talk to you," says Ragnar.

Fear burrows in my chest. Maybe I'm too late? But I'm careful not to show any signs of weakness. People like that see them right away, so I just glare at him coldly.

"If you've done something to her," I hiss. "If you have . . . if there is . . . I have to know that she is alive or I will start screaming."

Ragnar hesitates. He studies me, as if he is trying to judge whether he should take me seriously or not.

Then he turns his head and calls over his shoulder. "Ásta, come!"

My heart starts beating faster. I hear footsteps from inside the apartment, and then she appears behind him. It's hard to see her properly over his shoulder, so I stand on my toes.

"Ásta," I say. "Are you okay?"

She is pale and has dark circles under her eyes. The bruise has turned green and has oozed down her jaw.

"Look," says Ragnar triumphantly. "See, she's fine. She just doesn't want to talk to you. You're okay, right, Ásta? Go ahead. Tell her you're fine."

"I'm fine," says Ásta. But her voice is mechanical and low, and she doesn't look me in the eyes.

"Now you've seen her," says Ragnar. Then he slams the door in my face. I stand in front of the door, fists clenched. I can't go. I can't leave her there. But what can I do? I scan the area, spot an open window, and walk over to it. Inside is a small kitchen with an old stove and shabby interior. On the table are two spotted bananas and a carton of oat milk. I bend down to the open window and call:

"Ásta! Ásta, Io misses you so much!"

I wait for a moment, for a reaction, a movement, something to indicate that she's listening.

"Ásta, can you hear me? I'm worried that she's not eating enough. She's so sad! And what will happen to the kitten if she loses her milk?"

The front door flies open. I straighten up. Ragnar looms in the doorway, his face contorted with rage. "If you don't get out of here now, I'll call the police."

I stare at him. Making sure that I show no sign of fear, even though my heart beats frantically in my chest.

"Fucking cunt," he says. Then he goes back in and slams the door behind him.

I walk out of the garden. I pick up the phone, not realizing that my eyes have filled with tears until I see all the letters are blurred. I enter the number. Put the phone to my ear, listen to the sound when it rings.

"Jói?" I whisper through my sobs as he answers.

"I can't talk," he says, then hangs up.

18

I take a hot bath. I think about what Ásta told me about Planet Nine. I didn't have time to ask her before Ragnar stormed in, but I think she meant that Jói's wife was my ninth planet. The one I never see but still impacts my life every day. Ásta can't have known how accurate this comparison was. Because even though I decided to be honest, I didn't tell Ásta how often I look at his wife's Instagram. Ásta doesn't know how many videos of her I have watched, how I have studied the pictures she posts of herself and the children. I analyze them, listing her faults. One of her nostrils is bigger than the other. Her hair is much thinner on the right side than the left. Her neck is starting to wrinkle. She sometimes gets pimples on her chin.

She is not my ninth planet. She is the moon. Looming over me. Not always visible, but controlling the tides. And Jói is what, the sun?

I sigh and sink beneath the water, holding my breath as long as I can. I don't know enough about astronomy to make this metaphor work.

But this I know: I am *her* ninth planet. She has never seen me; she has no idea I exist. But I'm on my way, and I will shatter her perfect life in a shower of glowing meteors.

When the water starts to cool, I remove the plug from the bath, then stand up, dry myself, and wrap the towel around my wet hair. I put on moisturizer, put on my pajamas, sit on the sofa, and pick up the phone. I open Instagram, switch to my fake account, and find her page.

The oxygen in my chest turns to stone. It constricts my throat. My fingers go numb and I throw the phone like I've been burned.

I can't catch my breath. Black spots appear in my field of vision; I bend forward, putting my head between my legs and try to breathe. But the air doesn't want to move. I cough, and it's as if some reflex has been triggered and I can breathe again. I suck in the air, like someone drowning. The black spots recede. I straighten up, look at the phone lying on the couch next to me.

I'm afraid to pick it up. I have to pick it up.

I reach for it. Take a deep breath, look at the screen.

There she is. She is standing in front of a bookshelf in a tight white dress. Her blond hair is up in a careless bun. She's looking at the camera, smiling mischievously, her hands cupping her small round belly.

Under the picture it says: *Little one on the way!*

Below the heading is clearly more text. I press more, and there is a whole essay waiting for me. I scan it. *Been waiting so long, tried everything, repeated miscarriages, grief so deep. Didn't want to talk about it here, too painful. Still it's been a beautiful journey, brought us closer to each other, never lost hope. Then the miracle happened, our wish came true, wanted to tell you the truth, be honest, life is not always the glossy picture we show here. Thank you for your support, you mean so much to me.*

Then I notice that there are more pictures. I swipe. Her crying, holding a negative pregnancy test. Her injecting herself in the hip. She and Jói in an embrace. Her crying, her face hidden behind her hands, a large ring on her delicate ring finger. Then a sonogram, lying on a table next to a vase of flowers. The last picture is of them all together. It was apparently taken at the same time as the first one. She is wearing the white dress. Jói stands opposite her, his hand resting on her stomach, their foreheads touching, they looking into each other's eyes. In front of them are the other two children. Her arm around the boy, his around the girl.

I put the phone down. Go into the bathroom and throw up in the toilet.

19

I don't sleep all night. When my alarm goes off at ten to seven, I lie staring at the ceiling, still crying. I'm going to call in sick to work, and then I remember that I have a meeting scheduled with Þorvard. For a moment, I just want to say fuck him. But I can't.

I have to steel myself before I look in the mirror. But I still gasp. I look even shittier than I expected. I can't help but compare myself to the pictures I saw yesterday, the pictures I looked at again and again last night, as if I had been stabbed, but couldn't stop twisting the knife in the wound. How can she be crying and still so beautiful?

I look like I've been stung by bees. My skin is mottled red. My eyes are so swollen that they almost disappear in my face. Lips swollen, nose red.

I look at myself and start crying again.

Then I get ahold of myself. Open the bathroom cabinet and retrieve a pack of Sobril, an anxiety medication, which I keep there for emergencies. I wash my face and put on makeup as carefully as I can.

I feed Io, and when I go into the room to say goodbye to the kitten, I see that he's opened his eyes. They are light blue, like Ásta's.

My colleagues visibly react when they see me. I tell them that I had been invited out to dinner yesterday, had a severe allergic reaction, and spent the rest of the evening in the emergency room.

"Not a very romantic ending to a date," I say, laughing. "But don't worry, I'm on a strong allergy medicine! The strongest they have. Telfast? Sorry, no. Not that. Something stronger with more syllables. I don't remember what it's called; the package is at home. No, I have no idea what caused it. The lobster, maybe. Otherwise, the doctor said it could be anything."

Sobril, my anxiety medication, helps. And after lunch, the swelling around my eyes has subsided considerably.

I knock on Þorvard's office door at half past two.

"Come in," he calls.

He can't hide the look of surprise when he sees my face. But I briefly tell him the story I told everyone else. Eating out, allergies, ER, medicine, I'm fine! I smile as widely as I can.

"Good to hear," he says.

I take a seat across from him. He grabs his laptop and looks at it.

I've never noticed before, but he looks a bit like a walrus. For a moment I find the thought hilarious, but I manage to hold back my laughter. I took another Sobril at lunch, when I felt despair about to overcome me again. Maybe that wasn't a good idea. I've never taken two so close together before.

Þorvard clears his throat. Then he starts talking about Tumi. He confirms all the rumors that have been going around. Tumi is ill. Seriously ill. It's cancer, an aggressive cancer in a very bad place. He is undergoing rigorous chemotherapy, then surgery in Sweden, then radiation.

"That's terrible to hear," I say. "A man in his prime."

Þorvard nods, his expression serious. "I understand that the outlook is not particularly good. Of course, you hope for the best. But in any case, he will be out, at best, for seven to nine months. At worst . . ." He falls silent. Clears his throat. Starts over. "Maybe, someone will need to replace him as marketing manager."

I nod my head.

"That makes sense," I say, taking care to look thoughtful, as if I'm trying to imagine who could possibly take on this difficult job.

"We wanted to ask you to do it," says Þorvard.

"Me?" I say, pretending to be surprised. Very, very surprised. As if, even on my deathbed, I could never have hoped that they would choose me, the most capable and best educated person in the team, to succeed Tumi. It is so important to be modest—at least when you're a woman.

"Yes," he says. "You. You have good instincts, get good ideas. You are also a quick thinker. Balanced. If there are fires that need to be put out, you are the woman a man wants there."

"Thanks. That's so kind of you to say."

"There's also pressure from above." He winks at me. "About equalizing the gender ratio."

I smile as broadly as I can, until it strains my swollen cheeks. "I appreciate that."

"We'll increase your salary by twenty percent," he says.

"Up to the same salary Tumi had?"

Þorvard smiles. Holds out his hand. I look down as it hangs in the air between us. Þorvard's hand is large and tan and there is a wedding ring on its ring finger. I wonder if I would be able to chop it off in a single fluid swing with one of my knives. What kind of sound would it make hitting the floor? Would the blood ooze out from the stump, or would it squirt out to the rhythm of his beating heart? Would the fingers snap like carrots under the blade? I take Þorvard's hand. It is warm and it envelopes mine completely. He squeezes too hard, but I don't complain.

20

Io welcomes me when I get home. She purrs, twining against my legs, and nips me gently on the calf. I stroke her back, scratch her behind the ears and then sit on the sofa. She hops into my lap and begs for more scritches.

I want to call Jói and tell him the news. But I can't call Jói ever again.

I start to cry. I want to take another Sobril, but the one I took at lunch was the last one in the pack.

There is no one else who understands how long I have wanted this. Of course, I could call my mother, or my brother, and they would be happy for me, congratulate me, but they wouldn't really get what this means.

I want to call Ásta. I know she would be proud of me. I also just want to hear her voice, see her lovely smile, to know she is all right. But I can't call her, either. Fucking Ragnar.

It is unfair to finally make a friend only to lose her again.

I have wanted this for so long. And I wish I could feel some joy that it finally happened.

I wonder if I should maybe do something to celebrate anyway. Open a bottle of red wine. Order something good to eat. But I don't have any red wine, and the thought of walking down to the store is too much for me. So I just sit on the sofa, look at the ceiling, and let the tears roll down my cheeks.

My phone rings. I pick it up and the familiar thrill courses through my body when I see Jói's name on the screen. I am like Pavlov's dog. He has me properly trained.

I reject the call. Jói calls again. My body reacts again. I feel a sob rising in my chest. I want to tear out my nervous system, pluck out every single nerve that still holds faith in him.

I reject the call.

A moment later a message appears. I don't mean to read it, but it's already there on the screen and I can't help myself.

Unnur. My love. I am so sorry. I didn't mean for you to find out this way. This doesn't change anything between us.

I squeeze my eyes shut. Every inch of me hurts. My phone pings again as another message comes in.

Can we talk? I'm here.

I jump up from the couch as if I've been burned. And before I know it, I am at the living room window. And there on the pavement outside my house, bathed in a pool of soft golden light from a nearby lamppost, stands Jói.

We look at each other for a moment.

"Can I come in?" he asks quietly. But I can still hear him.

When I make no move, he adds, "Unnur, please. Let me explain."

I back away from the window. I feel like an animal caught in a trap. Could I climb out the bedroom window? Or are my hips too wide for the frame? Is the fall too high? What will I do if Jói is out there in the garden, waiting for me?

I hear his footsteps on the wooden stairs outside my front door.

My heart is pounding in my chest. I know the knock is coming, but I still feel sick when it does.

"Unnur," he says. "Unnur, please open the door."

I stand frozen in place.

"Unnur, please. Don't be like this. I just want to talk."

I walk into the kitchen as quietly as I can.

The front door is made of wood and is very old. As old as the house. It would be no match for Jói if he decides he wants to come inside.

"Unnur, please. I know you're there."

I say nothing.

My throat constricts, cutting off my air supply,

as I see the door handle going down. I glance at the kitchen sink. There is a knife on the draining board, the overhead light glints off the gray steel. The voice in the back of my mind screams at me to grab it. I am afraid of what I might do with it if Jói comes in, so I don't.

The door handle in the foyer is all the way down now, and then the door moves in the frame as Jói tests to see if it's locked. It is. The door handle moves slowly up. I can breathe again.

"Unnur, I didn't mean for you to find out this way. I wanted to be the one to tell you. I didn't know she was going to post this now. I love you. This changes nothing between us. Everything I told you is true. Unnur, please. I can explain everything. Please."

His voice cracks on the last word. Is he crying? I steel my heart against his pain. Cover it in armor.

"Go away," I croak, my voice barely more than a whisper. I clear my throat, try again. "Go away!"

"Unnur. Let me in. We'll talk this through. Please just let me explain."

"Go away, Jói, or I will call the police."

"Unnur, I know you don't mean that."

"Go away or I will call your wife."

There is silence on the other side of the door.

"Unnur . . ." he says, softly now. "Unnur, don't be like this."

"I mean it," I say, my voice shaking so much I am convinced he will hear that of course I don't.

Another moment of silence. I know he is weighing his options, wondering if he should call my bluff. But he evidently thinks better of it, because I hear footsteps on the wooden steps. They are slow, heavy. A moment later I hear a car door opening in the street and then slamming shut. An engine is turned on, and after a while the sound fades as the car drives away.

I sink to the floor and bury my face in my hands.

I don't know how much time has passed when there's another knock on the front door. I look up.

Io comes running out of the bedroom, tail high. She looks at me, meowing. I know her well enough to hear the questioning tone. *Are you going to open it?*

My heart lurches in my chest and then starts beating frantically as panic washes over me. Is he back?

There is a knock again, with even more fervor. Io runs into the foyer, then reappears in the kitchen doorway, meowing loudly. It's no longer a question; it's a command. *Open!*

I stand.

Io trots at my feet as I hesitantly edge closer to the entryway.

"Hello?" I say. "Who's there?"

"Unnur?" says a small voice on the other side of the door. A voice that I recognize.

I open the door.

Outside stands Ásta. She doesn't have a coat on in spite of the freezing night air, her blond hair is a mess, and her lower lip is split and bleeding.

21

I pull her into a hug. She takes a quick breath. I think she's crying, but then I realize I've hurt her. She's injured.

"Come on." I pull her inside.

Ásta bends down and takes Io in her arms. I can see she's trembling.

"I'll pour some tea," I say. "Go check on the kitten. He's opened his eyes."

"He has?" Her teeth are chattering.

"Yes. They're blue."

"Kitten eyes are always blue," she says. "Then they change color as they grow."

"I didn't know that."

She nods. Then she disappears toward the bedroom.

I run water into the electric kettle. Turn it on. Then I head out of the kitchen, grabbing a blanket from the couch on the way to the bedroom.

Ásta sits on the floor next to the cat bed, stroking the kitten. She's still shivering, and I'm starting to suspect that maybe it's something other than the cold. I spread the blanket over her. She smiles at me and I see blood on her teeth.

"Glad you came," I say. "It's going to be okay."

"Is it?" Her voice trembles.

"Yes," I say firmly. "I promise."

I go back into the kitchen, take out two cups, rummage through the tea drawer until I find the chamomile tea, and put a tea bag in each cup. I stand with my hand on my hip and wait for the water to boil.

I hear a loud banging on the front door. I jump. Jói must be back. But I'd locked the door behind Ásta. More knocking, then a crash. Something breaks. The front door slams open and a moment later Ragnar storms through the kitchen. He looks neither to the right nor to the left but stalks into the living room.

I hear a shout. Ásta. I run forward. Ragnar holds Ásta's arm; he's pulled her out of the bedroom. She is lying on the floor, her face disfigured from crying. She screams again. He lets go of her hand, kicking her with all his might.

I stand as if paralyzed. Watch him get down on one knee and punch her with a clenched fist.

It's like I'm floating. As if the air around me has turned to water. I move forward, reach out, grab a large statue that sits on the shelf above the TV. It is made of clay, but it stands on a large square plinth made of stone. I don't remember taking any steps, but somehow I'm beside them. Ásta is lying on her side, in a fetal position, curled up. Her eyes are wide with fear and blood is dripping from her mouth. Ragnar's head is in front of me. I can see that the hair on the back of his head is thinning a bit. I raise my arm, stretch it above my head. The statue is heavy, but I am focused. I target the spot where the hair is thinnest and hit with all my might.

22

Ragnar falls. He slumps, his head falling back on the seat of the sofa, as if he's decided to rest for a while, and then slides to the floor. I drop the statue. It falls with a thud. Next to me, I hear Ásta crawl to her feet. She is breathing heavily, as if she has been running a marathon.

Ragnar looks at me, then looks at Ásta. His face is full of surprise.

"What," he mumbles. He reaches behind himself, touches the back of his head. Then he brings his hand up to his face, unnecessarily close to his eyes, as if he can't see well.

There's blood on his fingers.

"Damn it," he says. Then he tries to stand. He is halfway up. It's like he's wasted but focused. I retreat. There's movement beside me. Ásta picks up the statue. She walks toward Ragnar, steps certain. She stops in front of him. He looks up.

"Ásta," he whispers.

Ásta lifts the statue. Ragnar shakes his head, tries to cover his face with a hand. But it's too late. Ásta drives the statue into his face. There is a crunch. When she lifts it back up, there's a crater in his forehead. He falls to the floor. Ásta stands above him and hits him over and over again until his face is a bloody pit.

23

I pour the tea.

24

When we finish our tea, I clear my throat. I am surprised by the calm that has settled over me. But perhaps I shouldn't be. This is the moment. The one I have been preparing for so long.

"Do you have your phone?" I ask.

"No."

"Does he have his phone?"

"I don't know."

"Can you check?"

We look into each other's eyes. Ásta's are uncertain; mine are not.

"Why?" Ásta finally asks.

"Just do it," I say, but nicely.

We leave the empty teacups on the kitchen table and go into the living room.

Ragnar is still lying on the floor in front of the sofa, where we left him. There is a pool of blood around his head, but it's smaller than I expected.

Ásta gets down on her knees next to the corpse. She starts by looking in his coat pockets and then in his pants pockets.

She looks up, shaking her head. "No phone."

"That's good. I know what we'll do."

She frowns. "We'll call the police, won't we?"

I shake my head.

"It was self-defense," says Ásta.

"Well . . ." I lean down to look at him, frowning a little. Ragnar's skull is concave. What was his face is now a pool of blood, as if his head is a bowl that someone has filled halfway. Light glitters on bone chips and something white that may have once been an eye.

I'm pretty sure those killed in self-defense usually don't look like Ragnar does now.

"He was going to kill me," says Ásta.

"I know. But I'm not sure the police will necessarily see it like that."

She looks at me. I see her thinking about it, coming to the same conclusion that I did while we drank our tea.

"What do you suggest?" she finally asks.

"Well," I say.

25

First, we drag Ragnar into the bathroom. Then I go into the living room and clean the blood off the floor while Ásta undresses him. Fortunately, I had the parquet refinished not that long ago. I only need to scrub where the blood has managed to coagulate at the shallow end of the puddle, but I can get it all. I eye the bloodstain on the white sofa, where Ragnar's head hit the seat. Stains set in quickly and I know it will probably be impossible to get out. But I can't order a new sofa right now. Something to deal with later, I tell myself.

I pour the bucket into the kitchen sink. The rag is pink with blood, but I rinse it again and again with soap and cold water until it's white.

I wipe my hands on the tea towel hanging on the stove, and then I grab the knife that lies on the draining board.

26

I make two trips down to the basement. First, I go to my storage locker and retrieve a roll of black garbage bags and two suitcases. Thankfully, my downstairs neighbor is on holiday in Tenerife. Second, I go to the communal storage room, which the condo association owns. Everything there is shared. Watering cans, hedge clippers, hoses, lawnmower, rakes, spades, and buckets. At every condo meeting we talk about organizing it, but somehow we never have.

It takes me a moment to spot it, but then I do. The saw hangs on a nail on the wall, deep in the storeroom. It's new, bought last summer, but it's never been used. I reach out, take it down. I hesitate. Then I grab the hedge clippers, too, before I turn off the lights and shut the door behind me.

27

Ragnar's body is now lying naked on the tiled bathroom floor. His clothes are in a pile under the sink.

Ásta is sitting on the toilet seat. Her face is pale.

"Are you okay?"

She nods. "I just feel a little sick."

I'm not surprised by that. I don't feel sick at all. Maybe that should surprise me, but it doesn't.

For some reason, in my imagination, I have always been on my own. It is much easier to have help.

"We need to lift him together," I say.

She nods.

I take the shower curtain down. Then I take Ragnar's shoulders, Ásta takes his legs, and we lift him into the bathtub. I am surprised by how heavy he is, though I shouldn't be. The expression "dead weight" had to come from somewhere. The corpse hasn't started to stiffen, so his bottom sags and hits the edge of the tub. We struggle as best we can, trying to lift him higher, and finally we get one hip up on the edge and roll him into the tub. He lands on his stomach.

Maybe it's better this way. Not having to look him in the face while we work. Or look at what's left of it.

This has always been the haziest part of the plan. I don't know much about the best way to butcher a carcass. But I do know that hunters always start by letting the animals bleed out. And it seems logical. It must be cleaner work when there's less blood.

I pick up two pairs of thin rubber gloves, the kind that doctors use. I have a bag of them; I've had them for years. I bought them at Melabúðin for Christmas after someone at work told me about wearing gloves when you cut smoked salmon so the smell doesn't stick to your fingers.

I hand a pair to Ásta. Then point to the floor, to the blood on the white tiles. These are not drops or puddles like before. This is sticky, as the blood has probably started to clot. Best to get it cleaned quickly. The true crime podcast I listen to did a whole episode on blood with a forensic specialist as a guest. There is a lot of protein in blood. And when that protein is exposed to air or heat it breaks and clots. Men often make the mistake of trying to wash bloodstains with warm water. But women know better. We have to. The heat only binds the blood tighter to the fabric, kind of like how boiling an egg makes it coagulate.

I pick up the knife lying on the bathroom sink. It's the sharpest one I have. This is Japanese steel. I bend over the corpse in the bathtub, slip the knife under its throat, and cut as deep as I can.

28

He bleeds less than I'd expected. Then I realize another thing hunters always do in movies and I hadn't taken into account. They hang the carcass up. Isn't that what they do in slaughterhouses, too? Let gravity help you? But there is no way for us to do that here. There is no hanger in the ceiling and I doubt we could lift him.

So I make deep cuts on his wrists as well. And on either side of his groin, where the large arteries are in the thighs. Of course, we can't google their exact location, because we've both read too many crime novels to leave a search history. So I take off my gloves, pull down my pants, and feel my own leg until I'm pretty sure where in my thigh the artery is.

I make long deep cuts, just in case.

The blood takes a long time to leak out. When we think the flow has stopped completely, I turn on the handheld showerhead and rinse the body. The smell of blood mixes with what must be the scent of Ragnar's aftershave. Or maybe it's the shampoo he uses.

Ásta vomits in the toilet. I still feel fine.

29

I grab his arm and try to lift him. But it's hard to get him up when he's in the tub.

"We need to turn him," I say to Ásta.

"Okay," she says, and then she grabs his other arm.

Ragnar's forearm is muscular and hairy. On the inside, just below the elbow joint, is a tattoo with old runes, which I can't read.

"Can you hold him up?" I ask.

Ásta grabs his palm. His fingernails are pale blue. She clasps him tightly, and for a moment it's as if they are holding hands.

I pick up the saw, position the serrated blade at his elbow, and start sawing. The first swipe tears through the skin. I pull it back, blood welling up in the wound. I push it back through, putting more weight on it now. The arm falls into the bathtub, the blood splashes on the wall, and I drop the saw.

"I'm sorry," Ásta whispers. "He's slippery."

"No problem," I say.

I open the bathroom cabinet and get the hair dryer. He's easier to grasp when I'm done.

When I've sawed through the muscles around the

joint, I get the knife. We put his arm on the edge of the bathtub, Ásta pulls it down, and I insert the tip of the knife into the joint and push as hard as I can. There is a crack as the tip slides in between the ligaments, but then it stays stuck there. I try to push the knife farther in, but nothing happens. I realize it probably would have been better to just saw through the bone above the joint. The tendons holding him together are no joke. Now the knife is stuck. I have to jiggle it back and forth for almost a minute before I can get it out. I hand Ásta the knife and reach again for the saw.

When the forearm finally comes off, Ásta wraps it in a black garbage bag. We are like a well-oiled machine, working in tandem as if we have done this a million times before. For a moment I feel almost proud of us, but then I push the thought away because we have work to do.

I have to fiddle with the shoulder a bit before I find the right spot, just above the joint. Then I put the blade to the pale skin and start sawing.

30

When my thighs and shins start to ache from crouching by the bathtub, I head into the kitchen and get a chair to set by the tub. It's hard work, but soon I get a good rhythm going.

The shoulder was more difficult than the elbow. I've learned my lesson and leave the hip alone, now going straight through the leg bone instead of the joint.

Io appears at the door and sniffs the air curiously. Her back twitches. She stares at the thing in the bathtub, then turns and silently pads back into the living room.

We decide to take the head off so the torso will pack better in the bags. The other option would have been to remove the feet and place them on either side of the head. I want it to fit neatly. I've always been very good at packing suitcases.

But my hands are tired and I don't want to mess with the ankles.

As I saw the neck apart, I wonder if the ankles might have been a better choice after all. The neck is full of cartilage, and the saw might be starting to lose its edge, because it crackles with every stroke, as if I'm skating over a rink that's breaking under me. Mom used to take us skating on the Reykjavík Pond when it froze over. Once, on a bright January day, when the sky was pink with golden clouds I skated too close to the northern end where the ice is thinner. I could feel it cracking under my weight as I skated back as fast as I could. I still have nightmares about plunging into the muddy water and being trapped under the ice.

When I put weight on the saw to get through what I think must be the trachea, air bubbles appear in the blood where Ragnar's mouth once was, as if he's trying to breathe.

Or maybe that's where the nose was. It's hard to tell.

It's easier than I expected to saw through the spine. The fine nerves glide under the blade like silk. I get through, and then all that's left is a thin layer of muscle and skin.

When the head finally comes off, I pick it up by the hair and hand it to Ásta. For a moment I see myself as I must look, like that statue of Perseus holding the head of Medusa.

Ásta is ready with a bag. One of Ragnar's eyes falls from its socket and droops on the thick cord of nerves. It appears burst, like an overripe tomato with most of the insides leaking out. Something gray and gelatinous falls to the floor. Ásta is quick to pick it up and put it in the bag. Then she wets some toilet paper and wipes the sticky pink residue off the tiles.

We know better than to cut into the torso itself. Inside are all kinds of viscera that we don't want to spill out.

We need to work together to lift his torso out of the bathtub. We balance him on the edge. Ásta holds the hairy chest while I open a garbage bag and put it around his lower end. Then we simply slide the body in.

We wrap more plastic bags around the body parts, sealing them thoroughly with masking tape. Then we arrange the pieces inside the two suitcases. They fit perfectly, if I do say so myself.

Ásta washes the knife and the saw while I clean the bathroom. I scrub the tub, first with cleaner and then with bleach, and I clean the stains and splatter off the walls.

I invite Ásta to take a shower first. Meanwhile, I find her some clean clothes, then run down to storage and put the saw back on the nail. I also return the clippers, which I ended up not using.

When I come up, Ásta is sitting at the kitchen table. Her hair is wet from the shower. The gym clothes I lent her are too big and hang on her like on a scarecrow.

"Do you want to try eating something while I'm in the shower?" I ask.

Ásta doesn't seem to be listening to me. She sits and stares into the darkness beyond the kitchen window.

I put a hand on her shoulder. She flinches and then looks up.

"I know you're tired," I say. "But we're not done yet. The only way out is through."

"I know," she says softly.

"Do you want to eat something? I have crispbread and cheese. And nuts. Maybe a banana?"

"No, thank you," says Ásta.

I nod. I understand. I don't have an appetite, either.

When I'm done showering, we put our clothes, Ragnar's clothes, and the gloves in a garbage bag.

I look at the clock. It's twenty minutes past two in the morning. Time to go.

"Ready?" I ask.

"Ready," says Ásta.

I loan Ásta a coat, then put on my own. We put on shoes and then leave the condo. It takes both of us to haul each suitcase down the stairs, but then we walk to the car, rolling the suitcases behind us normally like we're going away for a girl's holiday. Those budget airlines that always have you leaving before the break of dawn.

I open the trunk of my car. Together, we lift the bigger suitcase into the trunk. Then we put the other one in. I throw the plastic bag with the clothes in after them.

Ásta sits in the passenger seat. I get behind the wheel and start the car. The radio comes on; it's a song whose name I can't remember, something by ABBA. I pull away from the curb and drive off.

31

I let her out on Sólvallagata.

"You remember what you're going to pick up, right?" I ask. Because this is important.

"His phone, keys, and wallet," she says.

I nod my head. "And don't take your phone."

"I won't."

Ásta gets out of the car. I have my phone with me, but it's in airplane mode. I watch her walk to their house and disappear into the garden. I told her not to turn on any lights and she doesn't. One minute passes, then another, then a third. My heart beats a steady rhythm in my chest. I don't feel tired. I am wide-awake, more awake than I have been in years.

Then Ásta appears again. She walks over to a car, an old Toyota, and gets behind the wheel. The car revs up, the lights come on, and she drives off, turning left onto Hringbraut. I follow.

32

There are a few cars on the streets in Reykjavík, mostly taxis. Where are people going on a weekday at this time of night? There's more traffic on Reykjanesbraut. People who are really on their way to catch a flight. Ásta drives slowly through the lava fields. I keep a reasonable distance. An airport shuttle overtakes us. I hope it's not one of those that has a camera on the dashboard. But if we pull this off, no one will think to look at the footage. When we turn off the roundabout at the airport and head farther west, we are alone on the road.

Ásta puts on her blinker. She pulls to the side and stops.

I stop my car next to hers and roll down the window.

"I don't really know where to go," she says. "I've never been there before."

I think for a moment. "Okay . . . I'll take the lead. Just follow me."

I roll up the window and drive off. In the rearview mirror, I see Ásta following.

I hope there are no cameras here, either.

33

I turn into Garðurinn. The tiny village is asleep, all the lights off, so it seems almost abandoned. I spot sheep in a pen, surprised to see them out so late in the year. I drive to the two lighthouses, which are crouched at the end of the cape. One is small, old, and long since out of use; the other is also old, but still newer and taller, and lit. I stop the car. Ásta parks next to me. We step out. It's windier here than in town. I button my coat up to my neck.

We climb down to the shore. It's high tide and we stare out at the greedy sea.

"Do you have it?" I ask.

She shows me the phone. Then she throws it in as far as she can. I try to listen for the splash, but the waves drown it out.

"And his keys and wallet are in the car?"

She nods.

"Why here?" asks Ásta.

I look up at the sky, at the white twinkling stars.

"The currents. I heard somewhere that what goes into the water here will never wash ashore."

Still, I don't trust it as the place for the real disposal.

I don't know enough about currents to feel comfortable doing so, and tonight I will not leave anything up to chance.

Ásta blows her nose.

"Everything okay?" I ask.

"Yeah," she says. "I'm just cold."

I don't believe her. But I don't push. And besides, we don't have time.

"Come on. We need to find some rocks."

When we've found five good ones, we walk back to my Honda and put them in the trunk.

"Did you leave the key in the ignition?" I ask when we're both seated in my car.

"Yeah," says Ásta.

"Good." Then I start my car and drive off.

34

I drive along the Reykjanes Peninsula. On the right is the sea; on the left is a mossy lava field. It's like we're alone in the world. The road is empty and we see no signs of life anywhere. It's almost four o'clock in the morning when we pull into the parking lot at the Krýsuvík geothermal area. I'm relieved that it's empty. Not that I necessarily expected anyone to be here. But you never know with these tourists and when they might have the notion to go hunting for northern lights during their instagramable jaunt to Iceland.

I can't spot a single camera, which is good.

We get out of the car. The stench of sulfur in the air is strong and I can hear the hot springs. They rumble and the steam hisses like a cat.

I open the trunk, unzip the suitcases, and insert two stones into each. The fifth goes into the garbage bag with the clothes.

I parked as close to the hot springs as I could. Access here is good. There's a paved path that later becomes a boardwalk that crosses the hot spring area. But we're not going that far. The spring I have in mind is the one closest to the parking lot, and my suitcases are on wheels. I pull one of them and Ásta the other. The tires spin on the uneven asphalt and click as they go over gravel that probably crept in when it was last sanded for ice.

Ragnar is heavy, even though I'm pulling only half of him. I wonder how much he weighed. Seventy kilos? Eighty?

I came here with my mom and dad when I was thirteen years old. My dad was interested in geology and he had gone on about the area. I don't remember much of what he said because I didn't make a habit of listening to him when I was younger—something that I regret now. But I remember when he pointed out the scalding hot pool, told me it was full of sulfur and it would eat me to pieces if I fell in. I remember thinking that if I ever had to dispose of a body, I would do it there. The way I remember it, this was the first seed of my plan, the one it all grew from.

I guess it's possible that this memory, vivid though it is, is something that my brain fabricated later, trying to make sense of those awful days after he disappeared. When the hope of ever seeing him again had been slowly eroded by the certainty that he was gone. And yet I knew that although *he* was gone, *his body* must be somewhere. And there are so many ways to hide a body. There are so many places where no one ever looks.

I know that afternoon here by the geysers wasn't the last time that I spoke with my father. It wasn't until two days later that we woke up and found out he was gone. But it's the last conversation I ever remember having with him.

And I have been thinking about dead bodies and this scalding, sulfurous pool ever since. Although I never thought it would actually come to this, of course.

This is how life keeps surprising you. There are always unknowable, unseen forces at work. You make your careful plans, but at the same time the universe is hatching others.

I hear the pools before I see them. I stop, take the phone out of my pocket, and turn on the flashlight. It is dim, weakly illuminating the steam billowing from the hot spring area. The beam falls on red-yellow sand, white sulfur deposits, and green moss. Finally, it lands on a hard edge, beyond which is a white, dense plume of steam.

The hot spring is probably around two meters in diameter, but it's hard to tell exactly because it's blowing so much steam. But when the light glistens on the surface, you can see a gray, thick, bubbling mud full of sulfur.

I put my phone down on the sidewalk, directing the light so it illuminates our path.

"Grab the suitcase with me," I say.

I hear Ásta walking toward me and feel her lifting the other end of the bigger suitcase.

We step off the boardwalk and onto the porous

sand. This is treacherous territory, and I have no way of knowing if the ground will give way and my feet will sink into scalding water, but sometimes you just have to have faith.

35

I can smell the stink of it now. Feel the heat it gives off on my face and hear the lazy gurgling of the bubbles that keep rising and bursting. I wonder how hot it is. Three hundred degrees Celsius? Hotter than that? How long will it take the sulfur to eat through the bag, and the flesh, and the bones?

I'll probably never find out, because if everything goes my way, I'll never come back here.

We walk until we feel the sand start to give way under our feet, as close to the edge as we dare. I can feel the earth's heat through the soles of my shoes.

"Ready?" I ask Ásta.

"Ready," she says from inside the darkness.

We swing the suitcase once, twice. On the third swing, we let go and it flies toward the boiling hot spring.

The suitcase arcs through the air, then lands in the middle of it. The scalding mud splatters, but fortunately the muck doesn't reach us.

I hold my breath. For a moment it seems as if the suitcase is going to float on top of the mud. But then it starts to sink. Relief washes over me. We stand there until the last corner of the suitcase vanishes into the hot spring.

We retrace our steps, get the second suitcase from the car, and do it all over again.

I carry the plastic bag with the clothes by myself.

I watch it sink into the muddy water. As it disappears a tiredness washes over me.

But we are not done. Not yet. The only way out is through.

36

Ásta's face is deathly pale when we get back in the car. Her eyes are hollow and dark. I wonder how my own face looks. I feel as if this night should have added years to it. I think about the footsteps we left behind. How long it will take the wet ground to absorb them.

I tilt my head back, closing my eyes. This is my second sleepless night in a row. I know I can't sleep. Not yet. I'm just going to rest a bit before I start the car and drive back to the city.

My thoughts merge into a comfortable haze. But I startle awake when I hear a sound. At first, I think it's suppressed laughter. But then I realize that Ásta, who is sitting in the passenger seat next to me, has started to cry.

I reach toward her, wrapping my arms around her.

I can feel her bony shoulders through the thick coat. She is frighteningly thin.

"It's going to be okay," I say.

I can feel the weeping shake her.

"I . . ." she whispers between sobs. "I . . . I loved him, Unnur."

I stroke her blond hair, which still smells of my shampoo. "I know."

37

I let her out on Sólvallagata.

"You remember the plan, right?" Because this is important.

She looks at me. Her face is drawn, eyes red and puffy, with deep circles under them. But she nods, determination in her expression.

"I'll call him when it's morning. Then I let the day pass. Then I make a few calls, ask about him. Then I let the night pass, and the first thing I do when I wake up after that, is call the police."

"Exactly," I say. "Report the disappearance. Tell them his car is gone."

She nods. Then hesitates. "What if they find out that . . ."

I shake my head. "They won't find anything out. Don't worry, Ásta. It's going to be okay."

She looks at me with those big blue eyes. "You promise?"

"I promise."

"I just . . ." she begins, but then trails off. She bites her lip. "I'm just going to miss Io so much."

"I know," I say. "But I think it's best that we don't communicate for the next few months. Just in case."

She takes a deep breath. Then nods. "Okay."

"But I'll take good care of both of them."

"You promise?" she asks again.

"I promise."

Ásta gets out of the car. I watch her walk to their house and disappear into the garden. I told her not to turn on any lights and she doesn't.

I drive off, turning toward Ránargata.

38

It's ten minutes to six when I park outside my house, in the same spot where my car was before. Luckily, it stayed empty while we were away.

I take the coat I'd lent to Ásta, which was lying in the passenger seat next to me, and look around. When I'm sure I don't see anyone, I get out of the car.

I open the door to my home. Breathe in the smell of cleaning. I sniff the air. Is there a hint of blood mixed in with the strong artificial lemon scent? Or maybe I'm just imagining the metallic aroma because I think it should be there.

I close the door behind me and need to push hard because something bent when Ragnar forced it open. I need to take a closer look at it, but I don't have the energy right now. I have to change clothes, and then I have to put on makeup and fix my hair before I go to work.

Jói calls when I'm on my way to the office. I don't answer.

39

I go through the workday on autopilot. Get coffee, answer emails, smile, laugh at jokes, get more coffee, have two meetings. When I get home, I feed Io and then crawl straight into bed and sleep until eleven the next morning.

It's Saturday. I lie in bed and look up at the ceiling. I have cramps in my arms, back, and thighs. I think about Jói's child in his wife's belly; I think about my empty belly; I think about Ragnar, about the bags in the spring, about the footprints in the sand, about the phone that went into the sea. I think about the calm that settled over me as soon as I lifted that statue. That feeling of floating through water as I walked toward Ragnar and Ásta on the floor. Maybe I should feel bad about what we did, but I don't. It was either Ragnar or Ásta and we made the right choice. But I feel *something.* It takes me awhile to name the feeling, but finally I do. I feel proud. I have always known that I am at my best when under pressure. Especially if I have a plan. Now I've truly been tested, though I guess time will tell if my carefully constructed plan was a good one.

I get up, pour myself some coffee, eat breakfast, and

then I clean the whole apartment from top to bottom. I always clean on Saturdays.

I'm scrubbing the stain on the sofa when there's a knock. The stain is almost completely round, about the size of an egg, and it has proven as difficult as I'd imagined to get out of the white fabric.

I place a blanket over the stain, take off my scrubbing gloves, and open the door.

There are two police officers standing outside. The same ones as last time.

A familiar calm settles over me. I welcome it. It feels like seeing an old friend.

"Hello," I say.

"Do you have a moment?" asks the policewoman.

"Yes, sure," I say. "I'm just cleaning. I always do on Saturdays."

"Can we come in?" she asks.

"If you take off your shoes," I say. "I just mopped."

They promise to do so and I let them in.

I sit down on top of the blanket covering the stain. They sit in the chairs. I ask if I can offer them something.

"No thanks," the policeman says.

"Then may I ask what this is about?"

The policewoman clears her throat. "It's about Ragnar Stefánsson. Who you called about, remember?"

I cover my mouth. "He hasn't . . . hasn't . . . Tell me that Ásta is okay!"

"No, it's nothing like that," she hastens to say. "Ásta is fine. But she's reported a missing person. He hasn't come home for two nights."

"Oh," I say, letting my shoulders sag.

"It's just a rule of thumb to check everything," she says. "And you had an association with him that was . . . not on good terms. So, we just wanted to see if you'd heard from him or seen him since the other day."

I take a deep breath.

Then nod. Then I tell them that I couldn't stop thinking about Ásta with this man. That I was so afraid he would do something to her, so I tried to contact her.

"And when she didn't answer, I went to their house."

The officer raises an eyebrow. Then he pulls out a small notepad. "When was that?"

I tell them.

"And you met him?"

I nod. Tell them I went and knocked. That he came to the door, then grabbed Ásta, intimidated her into saying everything was fine, and then slammed the door in my face. I tell them that I then went to the window and called out to her. That he had come out, shouted at me, and then slammed the door again. I tell them all this.

Because there are probably witnesses. Neighbors who would have heard the commotion and looked out the window. I mean, I know I would do that if something similar happened on my street.

He writes it all down. Then looks up at me. "And you haven't seen him or Ásta since?"

"No," I say, shaking my head.

"Okay."

The policewoman smiles at me. "Thanks, that's very helpful."

Clearing his throat, the policeman asks, "Can I use your bathroom?"

The rational part of my brain registers relief. *It's over,* whispers that voice in that back of my mind. *We will get away with this.* I silence it immediately. This is not the time or the place.

"Yes," I say. "Of course. It's just down the hall."

He gets up, and I watch him go into the bathroom, close the door behind him. I hear the click as he locks it. The sound is muffled, as if my ears are underwater.

I go over everything in my mind. I have cleaned high and low, and aired out the apartment. There can't be a spot I've missed, can there? Did I actually clean under the sink? Is there blood under there?

It takes me a moment to realize the policewoman is speaking.

I look at her.

"I'm sorry," I say. "What were you saying?"

"I was just saying that sometimes things like this work themselves out."

I frown. "What do you mean?"

She glances over her shoulder, as if checking that her colleague is really gone.

"It appears he was in debt," she says, lowering her voice. "Gambling debts. Drugs."

"Do you mean . . . ?" I whisper.

"Men who hit their wives are cowards," she says. "And when it comes down to it, some of them take the easy way out."

I stare at her. I don't know what to say.

I hear the bathroom door open. A moment later the policeman reappears.

"Thanks," he says with a smile. He looks at the policewoman.

"Yes," she says, standing up. "We're taking up enough of your time."

I also rise, but too fast and the blanket on the sofa slides down to the floor. I feel the blood draining from my face, but she just smiles at me. Shakes my hand. "Thanks for your help."

She turns to the officer and frowns. "Nonni, what's wrong?"

I look at him, too. He is staring at the couch. At the now-visible bloodstain on the white cover, where Ragnar had leaned his head. It's reddish brown and faded from all my scrubbing. But it does not look like spilled coffee.

I feel the blood freeze in my veins.

"What is this?" He looks at me, brow furrowed.

"Hey, Nonni," says the policewoman. She taps his upper arm. "I'm guessing that you've never been sitting around watching TV and suddenly started bleeding. Not all women are like clockwork."

Then she looks at me and rolls her eyes. "Men," she says with a sigh.

I squeeze out a laugh and roll my eyes, too. "Men."

The policeman, Nonni, blushes.

When the door closes behind them I almost feel like crying, but I don't.

40

In the afternoon, there is news on *Vísir*. I knew it would come; there're only about two or three people who go missing every year, and the police always ask the public for help. But still, seeing his face sends a cold jolt through me. In his picture, Ragnar is standing in a doorway wearing a white T-shirt and jeans. Anyone who has seen him is asked to inform the police.

There's also a segment at the end of the evening news.

I study his smirking face, trying not to visualize the bloody hollow it turned into. I look at his throat, remembering the feeling in my fingers as I sliced through his trachea, and hear the wet crackling again. I look at his hair, trying not to think about when I grabbed those dark locks and lifted his head from his torso, holding it up like Medusa's before I dropped it into a black garbage bag.

It's the first time that I wonder if Ragnar has any family. Because I remember watching a similar news story about my father. It might have even sounded exactly the same, word for word. Except for the name, of course. I remember looking from my father's smiling face on the

TV screen and turning to look at my mother. She was pale, her lips thin, her eyes stricken. And I couldn't help but wonder if there was a hint of relief there, too. I never asked her if she had wanted him gone. I guess I don't want to know the answer.

I turn off the TV and open a bottle of red wine.

When I check the internet before bed, I see a little more news. His car has been found. The search has been stopped. I stare at the words at the bottom of the screen.

There is no evidence to suggest foul play.

I hide my face in my hands. Breathe deeply.

41

Weeks pass. The kitten grows at an alarming rate. Soon, he is running around the apartment like wildfire. He scratches my white couch, but I don't care. I'm going to get rid of it anyway. The couch, I mean. Because it was as I suspected; it's impossible to fully get the bloodstain out. But I'm going to wait until the kitten has calmed down.

It's so funny how he can be full of energy one moment and then sleeping like the dead the next. Almost like someone flipping a switch. One time he was trying to attack my toes—my slippers are open toe, and he can't leave me alone when I'm wearing them. And he fell asleep with my big toe in his mouth.

When he turns twelve weeks old, I take him for vaccinations.

He cries a bit when he gets his shots, but is otherwise incredibly brave.

"Should we microchip him?" asks the vet.

"Sure," I say. "I guess that's best."

The vet goes and gets some gadget. Then she stabs the kitten again, this time on the back of the neck. He doesn't cry this time.

Then she opens the computer and types something in. "Do you remember when he was born?" she asks.

I definitely remember that.

"And what's his name?"

"He . . ." I swallow. And then I say his name for the first time. "His name is Gestur." My little guest.

It's been a few weeks since I thought of that. For he may have come uninvited, but he is welcome.

The vet smiles.

"A special name," she says. "For a cat."

"This is a special cat," I say, stroking his silky black fur.

42

Months pass. Then it's Christmas. On New Years Eve, I give the cats lobster and cream. Io is calm about the fireworks, but Gestur doesn't know where the thunder is coming from.

January is dark. February is cold.

Life without Jói is strange. But in some odd way, it's also just the way it always has been. There's a void in my life, but maybe it was there before. Maybe I was just an ass to think that Jói could fill it.

Their child is born. It is incredibly beautiful, with a tiny nose and long eyelashes. I'm sure they could make a lot of money if they let it play in commercials.

I feel bitter, and I wish upon Jói a variety of unhappinesses. But not for his wife. Is that weird?

I have thought a lot. About responsibility. About guilt. About duties. About justice. About honesty.

I have also thought about the ninth planet. When she passed by in her giant orbit and shattered life on Earth in a shower of glowing meteors.

I've also been reading. And one of the things I've learned is that if the dinosaurs hadn't died, the mammals would never have had the opportunity to develop the way they did.

If the dinosaurs had not died, there would be no bears, no whales, no elephants, no monkeys, no wolves, no lions. There would be no domestic cats. No people. No Io, no Gestur, no Unnur, no Ásta.

Planet Nine destroyed the earth, but life went on. Sometimes it's good to let go of the dead weight holding us back, break everything, and start over.

That's what I've been thinking.

43

The three of us are sitting up on my new sofa when there's a knock. I'm watching TV, Io is washing her paws, and Gestur is nibbling on my toes.

Io jumps to her feet and runs to the kitchen. Then she looks at me and meows. There's a question in her tone. *Are you going to open it?*

I carefully extract my foot, releasing it from Gestur's needle-sharp claws, and stand up.

Io purrs at my feet as I walk to the front door.

I open it.

Outside, stands Ásta.

Her blond hair is pulled up into a messy bun on her head. She is pale, with circles under her eyes, but there's a smile on her lips.

"Ásta," I say.

"Can we come in?" she asks.

"We?"

I peer over her shoulder but see no one else.

The smile on her face widens. She slides open her coat.

I gasp. Then I hug her and whisper: "Of course you're welcome."

ACKNOWLEDGMENTS

Every writer needs a patient doctor on hand to answer all their weird questions. I am lucky enough that my trusted Icelandic editor and friend, Guðrún Lára Pétursdóttir, happens to be married to one. His name is Einar Þór Þórarinsson and I truly could not have written this book without him. Thank you, Einar and Guðrún Lára! Thank you also to Lóa Bára Magnúsdóttir, Rún Knútsdóttir, Alexander Dan Vilhjálmsson, and Fjóla Kristín Guðmundsdóttir for reading this book in manuscript.

Thank you to Lindsey Hall and Kristin Temple, my untiring editors, for your enthusiasm, care, and thought. I could not be in better hands. Thank you to all the rest of the team at Nightfire: Aislyn Fredsall, Hannah Smoot, Jocelyn Bright, Michael Dudding, Valeria Castorena, Isabella Narvaez, Greg Collins, Jamie Stafford-Hill, Rafal Gibek, Jim Kapp, and Jeff LaSala. I am so lucky that my books found a home with you!

Thank you to my amazing agent, Seth Fishman, to whom I probably send way too many emails.

And finally, thank you to Mary Robinette Kowal. It

is both a joy and a privilege to get to work with you on bringing my books out into the big world. Takk, mín kæra!

Hildur

ABOUT THE AUTHOR

Davíð Þór

Hildur Knútsdóttir was born in Reykjavík, Iceland, in 1984. She has lived in Spain, Germany, and Taiwan, and studied literature and creative writing at the University of Iceland. She writes fiction both for adults and teenagers, as well as short fiction, plays, and screenplays. Knútsdóttir is known for her evocative fantastical fiction and spine-chilling horror. *The Night Guest* was her first book translated into English. She lives in Reykjavík with her husband, their two daughters, and a dog called Uggi.

ABOUT THE TRANSLATOR

MARY ROBINETTE KOWAL is the author of *The Spare Man*, *Ghost Talkers*, the Glamourist Histories series, and the Lady Astronaut Universe. She is part of the award-winning podcast *Writing Excuses* and a four-time Hugo Award winner. Her short fiction appears in *Uncanny*, *Reactor*, and *Asimov's Science Fiction*. She lived in Iceland while performing for *LazyTown* (CBS) as a professional puppeteer. *The Night Guest* was her first work of translation.